# ON THE RUN WITH A CAPTIVE GUNMAN!

"They're catching up with us, Speedy!" shouted Wilson. "Do you see?"

The last frantic question was like a bullet kicking up the dust of the road before them.

"Pull down to a trot for this grade," Speedy ordered calmly.

And Wilson, overcome by a wave of horror and awe, obeyed in spite of himself.

All the rest had been nothing, compared with the time they spent trotting their horses up that grade, while a host of yelling demons flogged and spurred their frantic horses after them, and Dupray rode with his head turned, fiercely devouring that hope.

Was he, Wilson, a man who loved danger? Never, if danger meant this kind of action. He hardly knew what he was doing as he put the spurs into the tender flanks of his horse...

He pulled back to a hand gallop, and then saw Speedy and Dupray.

Behind them, hardly a moment away, came the others, charging. And every rider was firing as he came!

D0666783

# Warner Books by
# MAX BRAND

# LAWLESS LAND

## Max Brand

WARNER BOOKS

A Warner Communications Company

*Lawless Land* is comprised of the following stories, which were originally published in *Western Story Magazine:* "Speedy's Crystal Cave," "Red Rock's Secret," and "Speedy's Bargain."

WARNER BOOKS EDITION

This Warner Books Edition is published by arrangement with Dodd, Mead & Company

Warner Books, Inc.
666 Fifth Avenue
New York, N.Y. 10103

A Warner Communications Company

Printed in the United States of America

First Warner Books Printing: December, 1984

10 9 8 7 6 5 4 3 2 1

# Part One

# 1

Council Flat was one of those railway stops in the West where it seems that the planners of the road have grown tired of stretching the steel rails straight across league after league of desert and have marked with a cross the place where a little station house covered with brown paint shall arise. It is merely to please their fancy, and not out of any necessity or possible use, it appears, that they have built the place, and there it stands, to make a brief blur before the eyes of transcontinental passengers, shooting past.

No road led down to the station house of Council Flat; there were only three winding trails which, uniting a short distance from the station, led up to it, still winding slightly and without reason over the perfectly level surface. Beyond the point of junction, still meandering as though over rough and smooth ground, the trails separated and wound away into a distant horizon.

Inside the station, there were three people who had already waited an hour for a train that was two hours late. The middle-aged man was one Benjamin Thomas, and the girl who accompanied him was Jessica Fenton. The big young man, with the rather stylish clothes and fastidious, supercilious manner, was John Wilson. And the three had a common destination in the mountains that were turning from brown to blue in the milder light of the late afternoon.

That destination was Trout Lake, in the middle of those brown-blue mountains. Since they were all bound for the place, the talk turned chiefly on the tales that had come down out of the hills about the gold strikes and of the three hundred dollar "pans" that had been washed at the side of Trout Lake itself, and all around the creeks that wandered down into it through the forest.

They were in the midst of this talk when they heard the thunder of a train. It could not be their own, which was not due for another hour to come, but they went out and stared hopelessly toward the small spot that was swelling out of the horizon, seeming to grow larger without actually drawing nearer.

It grew so slowly before the eye that it was apparent almost at once that it was merely a freight train. Swaying and snorting, the engine went roaring by finally. The whole train was lost within the thin cloud of dust that whirled up behind it. Then it appeared again, as a small black spot. Finally it was gone.

It was about this time that the girl, whose eye was quicker than the others, saw an odd fellow come out of the bush on the farther side of the track. He was enough to set people staring in any community, because he was dressed in a long robe of silk, striped with red and yellow, and he had on his head a red and yellow turban-shaped cap of the same material, and there were red and yellow slippers on his feet. This attire gave him the appearance of an Oriental. His face, too, and his eyes were dark. One immediately placed him among more ancient races. Furthermore, his face was so delicately cut it looked less like flesh and blood than a statue chiseled out of marble. Yet, with all this, it was a face not lacking in decision.

This fellow, as he came up to the station platform, saluted the others by crossing both hands on his breast and bowing low, so that the tassel of his silken cap fell forward. The manner of the others in answering the greeting was characteristic. Young John Wilson started to part his lips, started to raise his hand, but, instead of doing either, simply nodded curtly without uttering a sound. The other man, Benjamin Thomas, was so surprised at the bow that he actually put his hand up to the brim of his hat to lift it, but recovered himself in time to turn the gesture into a salute. The girl looked at the dark-faced stranger with a smile and gave him a pleasant good afternoon.

He straightened from his bow and went on through the door of the station house.

After he had gone, the other three looked at one another. Mr. Thomas shrugged his shoulders and winked one eye expressively, as though this were a question that he knew all about, though he was holding his tongue. John Wilson had a faint glimmer in his eyes, but immediately afterward relapsed into his high-headed, supercilious attitude. But the girl said: "That's a wonderful face. Let's go look at him, if we can manage it without being too rude."

She was first through the door of the station house, followed by the others. They found that the stranger was seated, crosslegged, on a bench on the opposite side of the room. The light came in over each of his shoulders and showed him engaged in an occupation which was even stranger than his appearance. He had a small crystal, about two inches across, spinning on the upright tip of the forefinger of his left hand, and while it spun, the finger never wavered to one side or the other, yet the crystal kept its balance as though it were fastened by a rod through the center of the finger bone.

While it whirled and flashed, the stranger kept his downward look upon it with the look of a Hindu devotee—that is to say, with an expression of stony but breathless absorption. One might have said that this odd ceremony was some sort of religious pantomime.

Ben Thomas crinkled his eyes, critically, as though he were looking straight through the performance. Then he shrugged his thick, athletic shoulders, and leaned back in his place.

John Wilson stared, lost his supercilious look, resumed it again, and also leaned back.

But the girl crossed the room and stood before the stranger.

"We're terribly curious about that spinning crystal," she said. "I wonder if you don't expect us to be?"

# 2

The beauty of a cat lies half in its movements. Your dog is full of effort, tug and strain, when it is jumping about. But a cat will get up out of a sound sleep, slope from the branch of a tree to the ground, and nail a squirrel as it comes out of its hole all in a half second. The cat always seems to be folded up in utter repose, but it unfolds with wonderful ease. It is always loaded for trouble; it sleeps no more than a gun does. There is always a trigger finger ready to exert pressure.

As a cat slides from sleep into waking, so the man in red and yellow rose from the bench and the crystal ball disappeared in a flash from the tip of his finger. He was gravely attentive to the girl before him.

"That is my business," he said. "I am a crystal gazer, and I make my living by looking into glass."

"Oh, you're a fortune teller?" said she.

"Fortune teller?" said he, in a voice whose silken gentleness matched the beauty of his face. "Well, I am rather a reader of the past than of the future, but I see something of the future, also. But shadows of light are harder to decipher than shadows of darkness."

"I don't understand that," said Ben Thomas, drawing nearer.

John Wilson also drifted toward them, maintaining his aloof air, as though his feet were bearing him forward without the intervention of his will.

"Why," said the girl, "I suppose he means that he looks at the future as that part which has the light, and the past is the part which throws the shadow."

"Eh? Maybe, maybe!" said Ben Thomas. "What's your country, stranger?"

"I come from the country of Kush," said the other, "from above the Fifth Cataract, and the Oasis of El Badir."

"Cataract—that refers to the Nile, I suppose?" said the girl.

"It does," said the solemn crystal gazer.

He had been standing with lowered eyes all this time. Now he suddenly looked straight at the girl. She straightened a little, astonished at the sight of those remarkable eyes.

"Then you're an Egyptian. Is that it?" asked Ben Thomas.

"I am an Ethiopian," said the other.

"Well, this crystal gazing," said Ben Thomas, who was a practical man. "How d'you go about it?"

"I look for you into the crystal as it turns," said the youth.

"And what's the price?" asked the practical man.

His companion glanced at him with a sudden shadow of distaste in her eyes. "Whatever you wish to give me, so long as it is silver," said the man from Ethiopia.

"Well, a dime's silver," said hardminded Ben Thomas.

"That, also, is enough," said the stranger.

"All right, start in crystal gazing, then," said Ben Thomas. "And here's the dime."

He chuckled as he drew a fistful of silver from his pocket and produced a dime between thumb and forefinger.

The youth shook his head. "Afterward," said he. "There will be time to pay, after I have finished looking in the crystal. It is not I, but the crystal that speaks; sometimes I am too dull to understand it. In the end, if you have found some truth in what I say, you may pay me as you will, or not."

He finished, and waited.

"That's a good dodge, too," said Ben Thomas. "Nobody'll refuse a coin to a fellow with a game like that. Go on, then, and start the ball spinning, if that's the way you go about it. Then you can tell me what you see. I'm gonna learn," he continued, looking toward the girl and John Wilson, "that I'm a man with two legs and two hands, a heart and a pair of lungs. I'll find out that there's been a woman in my past and there's gonna be a woman in my future. Oh, I know the kind of tripe that the fortune tellers give out. But we gotta have some way to waste the time. You go right ahead, sonny!"

And he laughed.

Suddenly in the hand of the man from Ethiopia there again appeared the crystal ball, and he raised it until it stood on the tip of his delicately tapering forefinger, at such a height that it was between his eyes and those of Ben Thomas.

"You are ready," said he. "And therefore—"

He flicked the ball with his right hand, and it began to whirl rapidly about, with a flicker of reflected sunshine trembling in its depths. The face of the Ethiopian turned to stone; all life died out of his eyes, as they stared.

He spoke, and his voice was a dead, wooden thing.

"In the past there is a red shadow, and in the future there is a red light."

"What kind of red? Paint? Or whiskey?" asked Ben Thomas. The heavy lines of his face wreathed in a smile and his mustache bristled with pleasure.

"Blood!" said the youth.

"Hello, there!" exclaimed Thomas. "Blood? I've been a butcher, eh?"

"Of men," said the youth.

"What say?" exclaimed Thomas. "What's the idea in this here? Trying to get more coin out of me by—by pretending that you—Look here, young fellow!"

He reached out to grasp the arm of the Ethiopian, the arm that was supporting the whirling crystal ball.

The arm disappeared smoothly, but not abruptly. The crystal ball was gone at the same instant, and the Ethiopian stood before Ben Thomas with his eyes on the floor.

"What sort of bunk is this, young fellow?" asked Thomas.

"Uncle Ben," protested the girl, "you asked him to play his game. You mustn't be angry with him for the way he plays it."

"I'm gonna find out something," cried Thomas.

His voice rose to an angry roar.

"Look me in the eye and tell me where you get that stuff about blood in my past?"

"From the crystal, sir," said the mild-voiced youth.

"Hey? Oh, rot!" exclaimed Ben Thomas.

He was an angry man, indeed; in the swelling of his rage it seemed as though he were about to lay violent hands upon the smaller man. But the Ethiopian, slender, erect, immobile, kept a blank but fearless stare fixed upon the face of the rancher.

"Suppose that the crystal should have told him something about the days when—" began the girl.

"Bosh!" said Ben Thomas. "You know me, and you've heard yarns about the vigilante days. That's it."

"No, sir," said the crystal gazer. "I heard nothing about you. I give you my word that I never have seen you before today."

"I don't believe it," muttered Ben Thomas. "But—"

"He talked about the past, but he talked about the future, too," remembered John Wilson, aloud.

Ben Thomas jerked his head toward the big young man.

"Yeah, and that's true, too," he said. "Whacha mean about the future?" he added, whirling back on the Ethiopian.

"Sir," said the youth, "the crystal sees not only the deed but the mind. It sees the red of blood in your mind."

"Well, now, I'll be—" began the rancher.

He checked himself.

"I've half a mind," he declared, losing control of himself, "to teach you to—"

The hand of the girl on his arm quieted him. He shrugged his shoulders and turned away. "Never heard such bosh in all my life," he declared.

"There is the silver, then," said the Ethiopian. "You pay, but only if you are satisfied."

"I've got ten cents' worth of heat out of your lying," said Thomas. "Take it!"

He threw the dime on the floor.

The Ethiopian leaned with an unhurried movement that was swifter and surer than the dropping of a bird's head to pick up a seed. The coin that had rolled in a flash across the floor disappeared under the shadow of his hand. He straightened again, unperturbed.

John Wilson said: "I'd like you to try with me, if you please?"

He flushed a little as he said it, and strode up before the smaller man.

"Thank you," said the crystal gazer. "I hope that there will be something to reward your faith, sir. Are you ready?"

"Yes, quite ready," said John Wilson.

He turned a deprecating smile and shrug toward the girl, as

though to assure her that he took no stock, of course, in this sort of thing, but was merely trying to make up for the atrociously bad manners of the other man. He was met by a glow of approval in her eyes that made him glance hastily away again, flushing.

The blank, sightless eyes of the gazer were now again considering the winking lights inside the ball of crystal.

"There is a coldness, sir," said the dull voice of the Ethiopian. "There is a coldness which fills my mind from the crystal."

"What coldness?" asked John Wilson.

"It is fear," said the gazer.

"Fear?" said Wilson. "Fear of what?"

"That I cannot see. But there has been much fear about you, and fear in you—fear for its own sake, I should say."

The color rushed out of the face of the big young man. He said nothing, but stared.

"In the past there is more strength than was needed," said the youth who watched the crystal. "In the future there will be enough strength, at least."

A shudder ran, uncontrollably, through the body of John Wilson.

"In the future, there will be strength?" said he haltingly.

The girl drew back a little, as though she felt that she were playing the part of an eavesdropper.

"There will be strength. There will be sufficient strength and sufficient trouble, also."

"Danger?" asked the big young man.

"Danger that you can avoid."

"And suppose that I do not avoid it?"

The crystal gazer remained silent for such a long moment that the turning of the crystal grew perceptibly slower and slower.

"If you do not avoid it, you still have strength enough," said the crystal gazer.

An exclamation burst from the lips of John Wilson, beyond his power to control.

"Thanks for that!" he gasped.

# 3

The voice of John Wilson was not loud, but there was a fervor in it that changed the whole atmosphere, and gave it significance.

He stepped hastily back and turning to the girl, in a way that showed that she had been constantly on his mind, he murmured: "I've made a fool of myself. I'm sorry. I've been an ass!"

She shook her head, regarding him, however, with a little constraint as she answered: "I know how it is. It gets on the nerves; it's like hypnotism, I dare say."

She smiled reassuringly at him, but he knew that inwardly she was despising his lack of control.

He was deeply flushed when he pulled a silver dollar from his pocket and dropped it into the hand of the crystal gazer.

The latter murmured his thanks, and he seemed about to sit down when the girl said:

"It's my turn. Let the crystal talk for me, too, if you please."

She stood before the Ethiopian, smiling a little, very steady of eye and assured of manner.

He, without a word, made the crystal spin again. "In the past there are only small shadows," said the gazer, in that silken voice which fell like an enchantment upon her. "Except one near shadow, out of which you have hardly stepped. A shadow of grief, a shadow of sorrow."

She caught her breath.

John Wilson, lingering shame-faced nearby, watched her hungrily. As he saw the words strike in, his own expression of protective concern spoke quiet volumes.

"You are still in the shadow, but it is not so deep. You are searching, and you are full of hope. You are walking forward into a bright light of questing. And there I see—"

He paused. The blankness left his eyes. A troubled frown appeared on that delicately modeled forehead.

The crystal turned no more. It disappeared into his flowing sleeves as he folded his arms once more.

"You still have something to say," said the girl. "You've been wonderfully right. There has been a great grief. And now I'm searching, and hoping to put an end to it. All that is quite true."

"Don't be such a gull, Jessica," snapped her guardian.

She raised her hand to stop him, and waited hungrily for the next words of the crystal gazer. Still the latter delayed. "I cannot tell," said he.

"You can," urged the girl. "If there's something ugly that you see, please let me know. I'm terribly interested. I find myself believing."

"There is one darkness of which I cannot speak," said the stranger.

The girl lost color. Then, nodding, she said: "You mean death?"

He looked straight at her, but he said nothing.

"Death?" she repeated. "Is that what you mean?"

It was plain that that face of stone would not give her a reply. The words would never be spoken.

Ben Thomas brushed in between now.

"I never heard such rot in my life," he exclaimed. "There's been a lot of nonsense about fear and strength, to our friend, Wilson, here. And blood, for me. Yeah, blood in the past and in the future. That sort of thing. Why, Jessica, I think that you half believe what the liar tells you!"

"Don't talk that way, Uncle Ben," said the girl. "I don't like it. It makes me unhappy."

She had brought out a dollar and slipped it into the hand of the Ethiopian.

"Wait a minute," said Ben Thomas. "I've got myself in hand. I just want to show up the silly fool. He's got a rigmarole, that's all. Look here, you! You say there's red blood in my future, eh?"

"So the crystal shows me," said the other.

"What kind of blood did you say it was?"

"The blood of murder," said the crystal gazer, with perfect calm.

An exclamation, as though from the force of a blow, escaped through the open lips of Ben Thomas.

"You dirty little hound!" said he, and struck hard, with the flat of his hand.

It missed the mark. The crystal gazer had slipped back a trifle, shifting his ground with the speed of a stepping cat, and his blank eyes were blank no longer, but filled with a curious light of pleasant contemplation, as he looked at Ben Thomas.

"Uncle Ben!" cried the girl.

"Mr. Thomas," began John Wilson, hurrying forward.

But the rage of Thomas had mastered him, at length, and now he lunged straight at the throat of the youth. "I'm gonna show him," he roared. "I'm gonna break—" He jumped back, suddenly, crying out: "He's broken my wrist!"

He was holding his right wrist with his other hand, and holding it hard, as he glared at the Ethiopian.

The girl had seen—but barely, because the movement had been almost too fast for the eye to follow. It was an upward stroke of the hand of the crystal gazer, so that the edge of the palm had struck straight under the wrist of her companion.

"I'm sorry," said the crystal gazer. "But I had to do something. I couldn't let him keep his gun hand intact until after I've left. But the wrist isn't broken. The tendons and the nerves are a bit numb. That's all."

Ben Thomas, panting with helpless rage, turned suddenly and rushed out into the open air, to let his passion dissolve. The distant rumble of an approaching train was growing louder.

And the crystal gazer calmly slid out of his silken robe, his turbanlike headgear, his striped slippers, and appeared before the others in ordinary clothes, with a deep-visored cap on his head.

He folded the clothes he had taken off. Being the sheerest silk, it was easy to make them disappear under his coat. But what seemed the chiefest miracle to the girl was the change in his appearance.

"You are no more an Ethiopian than I am," she said suddenly.

"Oh, certainly not," said he, "when I'm not in those clothes."

"If it was all a sham, it was a very good sham," she said. "I was believing, for a moment, that there was some occult power—oh, I was having a pretty bad moment!"

"And I was having a fairly good one," said John Wilson, shaking his head and sighing in turn.

"Why, you see," said the stranger, "everything that the Ethiopian told you had been told to him by the crystal and, of course, it was perfectly true. I wouldn't discredit fortune telling, if I were either of you!"

He shook his head, smiling cheerfully at them.

"Here's my train, now," said he.

"It's a freight," said John Wilson, as he and the girl followed him onto the platform.

"That's it," said the stranger. "I often use them. Lots more room on 'em than the passenger outfits. Good-by, and thank you both."

"Hold on," said Wilson. "I wish you'd tell me your name."

With that flashing smile that had newly appeared to take the place of his former Oriental solemnity, the stranger answered: "Why, people don't bother a great deal about my name. Nicknames are what they generally use for me. A great many call me Speedy."

"Speedy?" murmured the girl.

"Well," murmured Speedy, "the fact is that sometimes I've been accused of taking people for a ride, and that the riding generally is quite expensive. But don't believe a word of it! You'll find out that it isn't true!"

As he spoke, the second freight was thundering past the station, and into the dust cloud, into the uproar, he walked, turned, raced with the speed of a panther beside the hurtling train, swerved, and, pantherlike, jumped with feet and hands extended.

The next ladder down the side of a box car streaked under him; he grasped it and, as he swung back, holding by one hand, he took off his cap and waved to them.

The dust cloud swallowed him and the train, and the girl walked back into the station with John Wilson. Something led them toward the spot where the crystal gazer had stood and she, with a cry, ran forward and picked from the bench a shining silver dollar.

"Look!" she said, turning. Doubling her hand about the coin with a tight grip, she managed a wan smile.

"He said that I was to die!" she murmured. "And that's why he left my money behind him!"

# 4

Thomas was quite over his temper and full of apologies, before the train arrived. He apologized to the girl; he went to John Wilson and, as though shame and pain were fighting in him, he confessed the bad part that he had played, and laid it to the credit of an evil temper.

"I'll tell you what, Wilson," he said, "a wicked temper's a curse. I'm sorry that my poor father didn't beat it out of me when I was a youngster. There was that youngster, a bright lad, too, and I've sent him away thinking that I'm a skunk."

John Wilson was full of sympathy.

"It was too bad," he said. "But when a man's temper goes wrong, what's to be done? My father was a fellow with a temper, and he took the heart out of us children while we were still little."

His voice trailed away, and his eye hunted the distance.

He shook his head, finally, concluding: "It's too bad, that's all. And particularly because that fellow Speedy must be a man in a million."

"I think he is," said Ben Thomas. "He's a clever rogue, at least, and he's got magic in those hands of his. Did you see what he did?"

"No."

"Hit me under the tendons of the wrist with the edge of his hand, doggone him. That's what he did! Jujutsu, that's what he's a master of. You take one of those Jap experts, and they turn their bare hands into clubs, like they wasn't made of flesh and blood, but of iron."

"I've heard something about their tricks," said John Wilson. "They work on the nerve centers. Isn't that the idea? They paralyze the other fellow by hitting at just the right places."

"Yeah, that's it," said Thomas, sighing. "And that fellow Speedy, he hit at the nerve center, all right, when he hit me. My hand still tingles. Only, he made me mad, Wilson. Talking about blood and murder!"

"Why, I can guess how it was," said Wilson, "if you don't mind."

"I'd like to hear!" exclaimed the older man, eagerly. "Why d'you think that he talked like that?"

"Because you were just a little rough with him, at the beginning," said Wilson. "I suppose he got angry and decided—"

He paused, and Ben Thomas muttered: "Decided that if I wanted trouble he'd give me plenty of it. Was that it? Well, maybe you're right. I was thinking—"

His own voice trailed away, and there was still much distant thought in his eye when their train arrived at last. It was loaded with men and excitement, all bound for Trout Lake. In the coach they entered, they were only able to get separate places. But that hardly mattered, for the girl was soon in conversation with a cheerful young cowpuncher who had nothing in his mind except hope to make a quick million in the new diggings.

Ben Thomas, on the other hand, had beside him a leathery old veteran.

Like the younger men in the car, he was full of good cheer and high expectations. That was a perfect opening for the conversation which Ben Thomas wished to introduce. In five minutes, he had turned the conversation on the subject which was now nearest to his heart.

He said: "Somewhere or other out here, I've been hearin' about a fellow by name of Speedy, a queer fellow, and a queer name. Ever heard it?"

"Speedy?" repeated the other.

Suddenly he snapped his fingers.

"Hey, wait a minute," said he. "What kind of a looking gent do you mean?"

"Well," said Ben Thomas, "I'll tell you. The gent that I

seen was not so big, not more'n middle height. Not more'n a hundred and fifty or sixty pounds. Dark hair and eyes, and pretty well tanned up. Might've been a Mexican, or something, by the look of him, except that the eyes were different. Handsome, too, almost like a woman, he was so doggone good looking.''

"Yeah, that's Speedy, and he ain't no woman, neither," said the veteran.

He paused, to chuckle a moment.

"You know him?" asked Thomas.

"Me? I dunno that I can say that I know him. Nobody knows Speedy. I know some things about him, that's all. What was he doing?"

"Oh, spinnin' of a little crystal ball on the end of his finger, and telling lies about what he seen in it.''

"That's him," said the other. "Juggling things around is what he's always doing. I seen him, once, keep seven knives in the air, and sink 'em all in the same crack in the wall, when he finished.

"Juggling is his game. He don't throw knives into flesh, neither, unless he gets real pressed. And only a doggone fool would press Speedy. No, sir, he don't need no weapons, and he don't carry none—he's got his bare hands, and that's enough for him, no matter where he is.''

"What sort of a gent is he?" asked Thomas. "Kind of a loafer?"

"You said something that time," said the older man. "He never was knowed to do a lick of work.''

"Oh, just a thievin' tramp, eh?" asked Ben Thomas, rather relieved.

"Him? He tramps around, but he don't steal nothing, except from them that steals from others," declared the prospector.

"Now, whacha mean by that?"

"I mean what I say. If you was around Speedy, your money would be safe in your pocket, and so would mine. And if I was busted, I'd get a new stake from him, maybe, whether he knew me or not. He gives away like water, to gents that he knows.''

"Humph!" muttered Ben Thomas. "Where would he be getting his coin, then?"

"Suppose," said the prospector, leaning forward and marking off his points with a gnarled forefinger against a calloused palm, "suppose that you was a crook at cards, say, and stacked the deck, or worked the brakes on a roulette wheel, or something like that, and that you trimmed a lot of poor suckers for a thousand or so every day of your life."

"Go on," said Ben Thomas, greatly interested.

"Well," said the prospector, "if you was that kind, you wouldn't like to see Speedy come to play your game, because he'd be sure to beat you and the roulette wheel, too. He'd find ways. If you stacked the pack, he'd stack it better. If you tried tricks, he's got about a thousand tricks up his sleeve, and he's always ready to use 'em, too."

"Yeah?" muttered Ben Thomas thoughtfully.

"Them that don't make trouble for other folks don't have no trouble with Speedy," said the prospector, "but them that live on their guns and their wits, they're the meat for him. They're what he lives off of."

The prospector began to stir from side to side and laugh heartily.

In the meantime, the train was leaving the flat and entering the foothills of the mountains that held Trout Lake.

# 5

They reached the station nearest to Trout Lake well into the night; then they took the stage. In the dawn of the next day, they wound down into Trout Lake, a weary lot, but fighting weariness with the hopes they carried with them.

When the stage topped the last crest in the rose of the morning, they could see white-headed mountains shining in a bright sky, and mighty forests of pine trees robing the slopes darkly to the bottom of the valley. In the midst of the valley lay Trout Lake, sparkling with blue light.

The girl, who had slept a great part of the way, with her head sunk against the shoulder of John Wilson, wakened now and looked up first at the mountains and the sky, and then at the face of Wilson, raised above her.

She did not know, for a moment, where she was, and merely wondered, vaguely, at the rigid strength of the chin, thrusting forward, and at the pallor of the handsome face. Then she remembered, suddenly, and sat up, blinking.

"Rested?" asked John Wilson, rather huskily, for he had the chill of the long night drive in his throat.

"Yes, thanks to you," said she. "You ought to have waked me up. I've been leaning against you I don't know how long!"

"That's all right," said he. "I didn't mind."

He flushed a little, and at this the girl frowned slightly. She looked at Ben Thomas, sitting opposite her, big, burly, immovable as a rock, in spite of any discomforts of body or soul, and he gave her a brief salute.

John Wilson was saying: "You're thinking of something."

"Yes," said she.

Suddenly she turned and looked straight at him. "I was thinking of what Speedy said," she answered.

"About you?" said Wilson. "Oh, that was only a joke."

"It wasn't a joke," she answered. "And I wasn't thinking about that, either. I was remembering what he had said about you."

She was sorry, that moment, that she had spoken as she did, for she was remembering the exact words of Speedy as he told Wilson that there had been fear in his life and that his strength was greater than he thought.

She was sorry, because the proud face of her companion was drawn with pain instantly. But he answered at once: "You're right, and he was right. Fear! That's it. Fear! I—" He paused and locked his jaws together.

"More strength than you think. He said that, too," said the girl, quietly.

He did not look down at her. He did not need to, for she felt the tremor that ran through his body.

Then there were things to occupy them other than the contents of their minds, for the stage driver began to make his grand entrance into Trout Lake, which consisted in whipping up his six horses to a full gallop and taking the stage through twenty sharp curves and corners on the lower part of the road into the mining town. The trees rushed beside them in a solid blur. The cold air of the morning leaped at their faces in a strong gale, numbing them to the bone.

They clung to the sides of the coach and smiled faintly, with frozen lips, as though they were striving to enjoy this dangerous adventure.

She looked askance at big John Wilson and saw that his eyes were still abstracted, looking into the future.

If there was fear in him, it was not the sort of fear that was fed by the danger of six maddened horses rushing around the bends of a half-made mountain road! Again she changed her mind about him, suddenly and completely.

There was finer metal in him than she had thought. What was the mystery about him? Into what danger was he passing? Into what danger was she, also, moving? Or had the prediction of Speedy been mere foolish words of the professional fortune teller?

She did not think so. She had heard from Ben Thomas, by this time, the gist of his conversation with the prospector, and Speedy became a figure of even more consequence in her mind's eye.

At last, they rushed with the thunder of hoofs into the rosy gold of the sunrise and down the main street of Trout Lake.

Men were already moving about the streets. A sixteen-mule team was laboring through the deep dust, and two wagons, behind the animals, rocked among the ruts as the stage itself was rocking.

Everything was rough, but everything was purified with hope and the sweetness of the mountain air that went to the bottom of the lungs with every breath.

They dismounted. They were taken into the warmth of the single hotel and seated at a long board, where they ate venison steaks, and corn pone, and drank powerful black coffee, all at a prodigious price.

Her father's friend, "Uncle" Ben Thomas, seemed pleased

by all of this, but the face of John Wilson had not altered, except to grow more and more like pale stone, with a supercilious, meaningless smile engraved upon it. He, certainly, felt that he was closer to some hour of trial.

What could the trial be?

After breakfast, Ben Thomas hired a pair of saddle mules.

He and the girl mounted and were off, up the valley, with the clangor of work beginning and the sound of men's voices singing here and there, among the trees.

"It seems," she said suddenly to Ben Thomas, "as though nothing but good could be in the air, doesn't it, Uncle Ben? And yet—"

He filled in the pause.

"You're thinking about that fellow Speedy, eh? Aw, forget about that. He was only playing a game!"

"Do you think so?" she asked, but not as one who can be easily convinced.

"Well, look a-here," said Thomas, heartily, "you don't believe in the doggone crystal ball, do you?"

"Well, I suppose not," said she.

"Answer one way or the other. D'you, or don't you believe?"

At this, she finally shook her head.

"No," she admitted. "I don't really believe any of that."

"What's left then?" asked Ben Thomas.

"I don't know," said the girl. "Unless he were a sort of mind reader."

"What mind did he read to find you dead, Jessie?" asked the other, roughly.

"I don't know," she said.

"Just a lot of rot, and that kid, that Speedy, he knew how to do his tricks, and make it seem something real. That was all," said Ben Thomas, dismissing the whole idea. "Now, you take this— Hello, there's the place—"

"The two black rocks and the pine between 'em," cried the girl. "That's it! That's it!"

She hurried her mule into the lead down the trail, and at the same time a tall man in ragged clothes came out from behind

one of the rocks, and sent his cry of welcome ringing down
the valley toward them.

# 6

The tall man was Oliver Fenton, big and gaunt, as gray as
one of the huge mountains about them, and he carried in his
face a look that was partly savage and partly sad. For three
years he had been a hunted man because the death of Henry
Dodson had been laid to his account. Pursuit by man hunters
for three years is enough to whiten a man's hair and line his
face. But he was illumined with happiness as he held his
daughter close.

He turned from her to grip Ben Thomas by both arms,
making him tremble in the force of that grasp.

"There was nobody in the world that I could turn to,
Ben," said he, "but I knew that I could trust you. And I was
right. She's here, and you're with her, and it's the first happy
minute I've had in these three years. But get into the trees as
fast as you can. Nobody has found the diggings yet. Hurry,
man, hurry! I heard a horse neigh down the trail!"

They pushed on past the two black rocks, and then turned
sharply aside among the trees. Instantly they were climbing
over the most difficult sort of path. They had to dismount,
then sweat and toil up the ragged surface, leading their
mules.

For half an hour, at least, they struggled on up the mountainside, keeping their breath for the climbing, rather than for
talk.

Then, at the end of the climb, they came out into the
flattened shoulder of the mountain, to a small clearing. There
the trees stood back from a little trickle of water that widened
into a pool two steps across.

"This is the place," said Oliver Fenton. "This is the
place, Ben. I've been watching over it like a miser all these
weeks since I wrote to you. I knew when I tried the stuff that
it was a fortune. Look! Here's a pan. Wash out some of that

black stuff here—right here—yes, or anywhere along the creek, if you're to call that runlet a creek!"

Ben Thomas, frowning to disguise his eagerness, caught up the pan. Digging in the soft black clayey soil he scooped out some of the earth and washed it rapidly in the runlet. There remained in the pan, when he had finished, a little heap of golden grains and dust.

Thomas sifted it into his hand; it made a respectable little pyramid. "That's about eight or ten ounces," said Thomas, considering. He was like a man in a dream, looking before him, seeing wonders.

"Nearer to ten ounces. I take it," said Oliver Fenton.

He was smiling and nodding, not looking toward Thomas, but at his daughter; and she kept her own gaze fixed on Fenton, as though all this matter of the gold were a small thing to her.

"Take one long day of work," muttered Ben Thomas, "and a man, he could wash out the price of my whole ranch, and the cows that're on it—I mean, with the mortgage considered and all."

"A man could do that, Ben," agreed the fugitive.

"Look," said Thomas, huskily. "I've been and worked all my life, and look at what I've got. Nothin' but a bit of no-good land and a couple mangy cows!"

"You've got a good place, man," argued Fenton. "You've made a living out of it for a long time."

"I could've made a living breaking rocks, too," said Thomas. "It's been the sweat of my brow that's made the money, not the land. And here—here you take and wash the price of that doggone ranch out of the mud in one day."

He dragged down a great breath.

"Why, Ben," said Fenton, generously, clapping his hand upon the powerful shoulder of the other, "you can give up the ranching, now, if you're tired of it. You don't need to think that I'll forget that, in the pinch, I could turn to you? No, no, Ben. I'm going to make your fortune for you, along with ours. We'll split the thing three ways. One for Jessica, one for you, and one for me."

Ben Thomas did not seem to hear. He lifted his rugged

face, and a splotching of sunlight and thin shadow fell over it,
so that the eyes seemed to blaze like polished metal.

"What kind of Providence is there that they say watches
over things?" he asked. "I go and work hard and honest, half
a life, and here you come and wash out a fortune in a day.
That's what they mean by Providence!"

"Uncle Ben," said the girl, protesting. "Didn't you hear?
You're to have a full third share in it! Look! It means
millions, I suppose!"

"No, it won't mean that, hardly," said her father. "I've
washed up and down this creek. It's a mighty rich patch, but
the gold is all pooled in this shoulder, do you see? It's a rich
pool, but there's nothing higher up and there's nothing lower
down than this little plateau. Not millions. Maybe half a
million. Well, maybe a whole million, too. But at any rate
there's enough for all three of us."

He turned to the girl, and his eyes drank her in, slowly,
luxuriously.

"You've had a bad time, Jessica," he said. "Your mother's had a bad time, too."

"It hasn't been so bad," she answered.

"Not bad?" he exclaimed. "And you working out, washing,
sewing, teaching music, anything to keep soul and body
together? And you say that you haven't had a bad time? Your
mother, too, making a slave out of herself and your name
disgraced by me? You say that isn't a bad time?"

"We've never doubted you," replied the girl. "And the
rest was nothing."

"I'll clear myself one day," answered Fenton. "One day
I'll show that my hands are clean, after all. But now I can do
something for you, in a way. Here it is, in the ground, and
you go down to Trout Lake and file on this ground. File the
claim. Ben, take her down with you, will you? You know the
way, now. Stake it, and go down to Trout Lake. I can show
you the best places here. Stake for her, and stake for yourself.
Naturally, you can't stake for me.

"Ah, I've had nightmares, waiting here and watching.
Every day I heard voices somewhere near. They've prospected
the whole side of the mountain, I reckon. They'd've come
here, except that the run of water doesn't go on down the

slope. It ducks into the rocks, out of sight. But every day, I've been seeing the nightmare of some other man coming here, trying this ground, washing a handful of it and seeing— why, I've thought that I would be guilty of murder, if that happened.''

He turned to Thomas.

''You've found the place, Ben. We'll stake it, and then you start, will you? Start fast. We haven't any time to waste. Listen!''

He held up his hand. Far away they could hear the stir of voices coming faintly through the thin, pure mountain air.

Ben Thomas aroused himself from a trance and turned to the others.

''I'm ready,'' he muttered. And he added to himself, under his breath: ''Half a life of slavin'—and then this—just blundered onto!''

''And no one has seen you here?'' the girl was asking her father anxiously.

''Nobody. I've lived here like a wildcat in the shadow,'' he answered her.

Then he urged them on. ''Quick! Quick!'' he exclaimed. ''I'll be staying here in a sweat until you come back again. Stake it out, Ben. Here's the description written out, locating it. I know enough surveying for that. This is a description that will fit to a 'T.' Hurry along; I'll take you down as far as the trail!''

He escorted them away, a hand on the arm of the girl, a hand on the arm of his friend.

As they disappeared, among the shadows along the bough of a great pine that bordered the clearing, another shadow stirred, moved, sat erect—a man.

He was on the lowest bough and had been stretched there face downward. Now he climbed down, a considerable distance, with such surety, it seemed that he was possessed with claws, like a cat.

At the bottom, he sat down on one of the great roots that projected like the coil of a brown python from the ground and pulled on the shoes which had been slung about his neck. Then he stood up and stepped out of the shadow into the patch of sunlight that broke through the foliage above him.

Carefully he moved, never stepping upon the soft soil, but only from projecting rock to rock, until he came to the edge of the runlet.

There he stooped, scooped out a palmful of the earth, washed it with a gentle trundling motion, and looked down curiously at the glittering yellow grains of gold.

"Gold," murmured Speedy. "Yes, and murder, too. I guessed it before, and I know it now. Murder—red murder—the air's full of it!"

With quick glances he noted down the spot, and the guiding headlands that appeared, looming through or above the trees. When he had finished that quick survey, he could have found his way to this place even through the thickest darkness.

He was still lingering at the spot, when he heard other voices approaching, from the side, and at this he drew back as silently as a shadow that moves beneath a cloud across the surface of the earth.

The trees received him; the big trunks swarmed and thickened between him and the clearing, and so he moved back and back until he was at a sufficient distance to give over his caution and to stride boldly and freely away.

He did not walk, however. Walking was not for him, at such a time as this, for there were vital miles between him and Trout Lake, where he had much to do.

He broke into a run, as easy and lightly striding as the run of a Navajo Indian, those matchless desert runners that can put a hundred miles behind them between sunrise and sunset.

So, weaving among the trees, he sloped away across the mountainside, and as he ran he was smiling.

# 7

When Ben Thomas reached Trout Lake, his mind was entirely made up. He had been turning various possibilities over in his thoughts during the journey back, and his decision, he believed, was entirely practical. The moment he got to the town, therefore, he started to act on it.

He dropped the girl at the hotel, merely saying: "We have to hurry, Jessica. You have the mules put up—here's money to pay for 'em. I'll hurry over and arrange things at the bureau, so that there'll be nothing for you to do except to sign your name, when it comes to filing the claim. I'll be back here in a few minutes—maybe a half hour. Will you be ready?"

"Ready?" said the girl. "I'll be waiting on pins and needles. Do you know what it means to me?"

"It means a fortune in hard cash, or soft yaller gold, any way you look at it," suggested Ben Thomas, with a grin.

She shook her head.

"It means that there'll be enough money to hire one good lawyer, and I know that one good lawyer will be able to clear Father before the world."

He nodded, waved and was off, smiling reassurance at her over his shoulder.

As a matter of fact, her last remark had made him feel that what he was about to do was not a crime at all, but almost a virtue.

Who is it that does not know that lawyers are a quicksand that will swallow up a fortune as a shark swallows a small fish? Therefore, if the girl intended to spend her fortune on the law, it was far better that she should have no fortune to spend. That money would round out the sum that he needed.

He never had seen himself, satisfactorily, as a small rancher. The picture of Ben Thomas that he retained in his inmost mind's eye was of a great power, a man whose name would be familiar to the captains of finance.

He was sure that he had in him the brains and the mental resource to employ great good fortune, if ever it came his way. But the cattle business had not brought him luck. On the contrary, he seemed apt to buy high and sell low. Then there was the matter of the infernal mortgages. He had assured himself that in two years, at the most, he would be able to pay off the debt. As a matter of fact, he had increased his indebtedness, and never lowered it a penny.

In the back of his mind, there was established a sneering

contempt for most other men whom he met. He was always
seeing political posters along the roads, nailed or pasted up
and reading in place of the actual names: "Ben Thomas for
sheriff"; "Benjamin Thomas, the people's true friend, for
governor"; "The Honorable Benjamin Thomas, for the United States Senate!"

In those terms he saw himself, and they were the reality.
This actual self that moved through the world, unappreciated,
slapped upon the shoulder as hearty, hail-fellow-well-met,
Ben Thomas, the rancher, was merely the sham which bad
luck forced him to maintain against his will, against his
higher nature.

Now, as he walked rapidly down the street, he saw the
future with amazing clearness. There might be half a million,
perhaps a million in that black clay on the shoulder of the
mountain. Half of that sum he could put in investments and
he knew just where to place the money, in small loans to
ranches which would soon go under and whose owners could
be squeezed out into the road while he, Ben Thomas, proper-
ly organized the places. The other half he would use to pay
his debts, step forward as a public-spirited citizen, ready to
assume the burdens of legislation and law enforcement.

Well, he felt that he had the presence, for one thing, and
for another, he was confident that he had the brains.

This was the humor he was in, when he came to his
destination, a little shack on the street, with a shingle sticking
out over the door and painted with the inscription—Office of
the Sheriff: Samuel Hollis.

He turned in under the sign and found himself in a little
room, one half of which was clouded with the blue-brown of
cigarette smoke.

Through that cloud he saw a man whose hair was so
straw-colored, and whose eyes were so pale a gray that he
looked like an albino. There was something startling about
his nondescript features.

He was standing by a table and revealing himself in boots
and long, spoon-handled spurs. His chaps were of worn,
scarred leather, hanging over the back of a neighboring chair.
He was not very big, and he was not very impressive. Ben

Thomas wished that he had found a more formidable-looking man.

He stepped forward and said: "Are you Sam Hollis?"

"That's my name," said the other gently.

"I'm Ben Thomas. I've brought you news of Oliver Fenton."

"Ain't he the man that killed Henry Dodson?"

"That's the one. And he's the one that Mrs. Dodson will pay ten thousand dollars for, once he's brought to trial."

"Ten thousand is a lot of money," said the sheriff.

"I can tell you where to pick it up."

"You mean, where to pick up Fenton? Ain't that the idea that you're drivin' at?"

"That's the idea."

The sheriff nodded. "That'd be right friendly," he declared. A mild, childish interest began to flicker in his pale eyes.

"Here's the place," said the other.

Quickly he dictated the description of the way to the shoulder of the mountain where Oliver Fenton had struck the pay dirt.

"That sounds good to me," said the sheriff. "Maybe I could pick up that fellow. You don't know him?"

"I know him pretty well."

"Know whether he's much of a fighting man?"

"Every Fenton's a fightin' man," declared the rancher, "and Ollie Fenton ain't a youngster, but he's fast, and he's strong."

"I wasn't exactly talking about fist fighting," drawled the sheriff.

"He can use guns, too," said Ben Thomas. "He's a mighty good shot."

"He might be a good shot, but is he a cool head?" asked the sheriff.

"He's the coldest that you ever seen, when it comes to a pinch. He's the kind of fire that burns through steel plate like shingle wood."

"I've seen that kind of man, I reckon," said the sheriff, as mildly as before. "I'd kind of like to have a look at this Fenton, too. The ones that fight cold are always interesting. Show me a gent that has to warm himself up by swearing a little before he pulls a gun, and I'll mostly show you a gent that shoots crooked, too—unless he's Irish.''

He smiled a little, as he added the last words.

Thomas was satisfied. He was convinced that he was in touch with a man who knew his work. "You'd better take some others along with you," suggested Thomas.

"When I go out to bring in one man, I go alone," said the sheriff. "Now, about a split in the reward, if any reward turns up. Whacha think should be your split?"

"My split? Well, whacha say?" asked Thomas, always pleased to bargain.

"One third," said the sheriff.

"A half, sounds more like it to me," said Thomas.

"He's a fightin' man," said the sheriff. "I notice that you didn't bring him in yourself."

"Him? I couldn't bring him in myself, and I can't be mentioned. I know him, d'ye see?"

The eyes of the sheriff narrowed for a shooting instant.

"Might be that you're a friend of his?" he suggested.

"I ranched near him," said Thomas, uncomfortably.

The sheriff nodded. "I see," said he.

As he considered Thomas, the latter found that his face was rapidly growing very warm.

"We'll make it a half, if you say so," said the sheriff, half turning away.

"Aw, a third would do, too," said Thomas, red but amiable. "Let it go at that. And where's the bureau? I'm gonna file on a little claim—"

He reached, as he spoke, for the full description of the claim, which Oliver Fenton had written out and given to him. To his amazement, the papers were no longer in his coat pocket!

# 8

There was a reason for the disappearance of the prize from the pocket of big Ben Thomas.

When he reached the hotel with the girl, across the street, in the smoky mouth of a blacksmith shop, Speedy was standing, breathing rather hard from his long run across the uplands and through the woods. But he was content because he had arrived in town before Thomas and his protégée. It was not for nothing that he had lain out on the limb of the pine tree and studied the upturned evil in the face of the big man, back there in the clearing.

Now, eager and keen as a hunting hawk, he watched the girl take the two mules, while Thomas turned down the street.

Speedy was after him at once, and his movements were like the flight of a snipe downwind. For he did not go straight forward. Pursuing an irregular course, pausing here, halting there, and then cutting at a diagonal across the street, he came up behind his quarry just as Ben Thomas paused to allow an eight-mule team to turn in the street, the tossing heads of the leaders swinging across the sidewalk.

"Good work!" called Ben Thomas, cheerfully to the teamster, at that moment, and waved his hand.

As he waved and the wagon straightened out down the street, the coat of Ben Thomas belled out, and under the flap of the pocket Speedy could see the glint of white, the top edges of the papers.

His hand dipped in like the beak of a bird and came out again, bearing the prize, which disappeared into his own coat with such speed that even if any passer-by had been looking, he would have seen hardly more than a flash of light, as Speedy turned on his heel and hurried back up the street to the hotel.

Only once he paused and risked a glance behind him, and that glance showed him Ben Thomas turning in under the sheriff's sign!

It was enough to indicate that he needed speed, but he had to be nonchalant, also.

He went to the hotel clerk and asked for Miss Fenton. She would be called. The clerk himself went to do it, and a rusty-headed boy slid in behind the desk to take up the duties of handing out and receiving keys.

Through the register, the fingers of Speedy sifted, found that day's arrivals, and glanced at the handwriting of the girl.

A second and longer glance printed the characters in his mind, and the next moment he was writing a by no means clumsy imitation of her hand:

> DEAR UNCLE BEN: I've just seen an old friend, and he asked me to go down the street to see his father. I'll be back in a half hour or so. Wait for me here.
>
> JESSICA

He folded the paper and pushed it across the table to the red-headed boy. "Give this to Mr. Ben Thomas when he comes in, will you?" he asked.

"Sure," said the boy, and stuffed the paper into its keybox.

When Speedy turned, the clerk was coming toward him, and Jessica Fenton along with him.

There was first a shock of surprise in her face, followed at once by the most brilliant of smiles. Genuine pleasure made her hold out her hand and grip Speedy's.

"I might have known that you'd be traveling toward the most excitement," said she. "How are you, Speedy? Or do you really want people to call you that?"

"I can't help myself," said he. "I'm one of those poor chaps who can't keep a name of his own. I've tried all sorts of names, but they won't stick. I've brought you a message from Mr. Thomas."

"Oh, you've seen him?" asked the girl.

Trouble was in her eyes, the old trouble, as she watched her companion.

"We're not enemies," said Speedy, "because of that little trouble at Council Flat. Mr. Thomas was in a crush of business, something that he had to do at once. He begged me to do something for you and, of course, I said that I would."

He drew the papers from his pocket, and her eyes widened as she recognized the handwriting of her father.

"Here's the description of a claim that he wants you to hurry down to the bureau and file."

"But he has to go along and file with me," said the girl. "That's the agreement!"

"Is it?" said Speedy. He went on, smoothly: "Thomas doesn't want any part of the claim, according to what he says.

His idea is that if anything happens to him, well, people wouldn't know that he owed it all to you, and that it's really your property. He was only going to file to help you hold the property."

He had ended rather lamely on this note, but the girl had not the slightest suspicion in her mind.

"That's great-hearted!" she exclaimed.

"Well, he's a big man, and he has to have a heart that will match his size," said Speedy calmly. "We'd better start. He said that there was the greatest sort of a hurry."

"He was in a hurry," admitted the girl. "We'll go along. Do you know the way?"

"Yes."

He had, in fact, spotted the place on his first visit to the town. He was not one who could settle blindly into any nest, for the world was filled with enemies for Speedy, and he dared not close both eyes at once, either by night or day, in new surroundings or old ones.

He waved her on, and paused again for a moment to say to the clerk: "What's the sheriff look like?"

"You mean Sam Hollis?"

"Yes, of course."

"Why, you can't mistake Sam. Smallish, and ain't got no color in his hair and eyes, but Sam's a real man that'll—"

He broke off with a grunt, for Speedy was already gliding away to the door, where he joined the girl and turned down the street.

There was much for him to do, and, because of it and the danger that lay before him, he smiled and hummed as he walked along.

"This is a happy day for you," said the girl.

"It's the mountain air," he answered her. "It gives a fellow life."

She drew out a broad silver dollar and held it out.

"I owe you this," she said.

The happiness went out of his face and left it grim.

Then he shook his head: "I can't take it. Not yet!" said he.

It seemed to her that half the brightness went out of the morning. "Death" had been his word to her the day before,

and death, she felt, was in his expression again at this
moment.

They turned into a long, low shed, filled with smoke, from
which there issued an uproar of angry voices as half a dozen
men disputed before another man on the other side of a desk,
which was made of a flat board laid over two hurdles. The
man had a tired face.

"You see him?" said Speedy.

"Yes"

"He'll record the claim. It won't take long, once you get to
him. But I'll tell you something more, you want to get in
there as fast as you can. Shove in, Miss Fenton. Shove
straight ahead and try to close up the deal. I have to leave
you. These fellows will give way to you when they know that
you only have a half hour."

"A half hour," she asked him, with suddenly increased
interest. "What do you mean? Is there something that you're
keeping back from me?"

"Nothing that would do any good, if it were told," said
Speedy cheerfully, making his expression brighter for her
sake.

"But how can you know that there's exactly a half
hour?"

"It's something that I got out of this good clean mountain
air as I was coming down the street. It's just that I have a
pretty keen sense of time, d'you see?"

She eyed him, shaking her head.

What there was behind his words she could not, of course,
guess, but her mind groped blindly, striving for some clue.
Somehow, very strongly, she felt that Speedy was heading
into danger.

However, that would never be solved by her, and she
stepped forward into the waiting line.

Speedy, in the meantime, got into the street in time to see a
man dismount from a lump-headed yellow mustang, a fifty-
dollar antique, with a ten-dollar wreck of a saddle cinched on
its back.

"How much for that outfit?" he asked.

"To you, brother, only two hundred bucks," said the
other, grinning a little in the eyes, but not with the lips.

Two hundred dollars in currency was suddenly counted into his amazed hands.

"Hold on!" he exclaimed.

"See you later," said Speedy, and sprang into the saddle.

The Westerner watched him go down the street, bounding high with every stride of the mustang.

"Another doggone fool of a tenderfoot!" he said to himself, and began to count his money over again.

# 9

A mile up the ravine, Speedy, already well pounded and hammered by the clumsy gait of the mustang, passed another single horseman on the way, pushing his horse ahead at a steady, easy dogtrot.

As Speedy went by, he noted the pale hair, the paler eyes, the keenness of his glance, and something quietly efficient and self-reliant about the way the man sat his saddle. That was Sam Hollis, he could lay his bet, and if it were Hollis then there was still plenty of time to do the work that he had in mind.

He was glad to reduce the pace of the yellow mustang, therefore, and still he was reasonably sure that he had gained a good half mile on the man of the law by the time he came to the two black rocks with the evergreen tree between them.

He dismounted, led the horse, trailing and stumbling behind him for a short distance into the woods, tethered it there, and then went at full speed up the hillside.

He had gone on for some distance before he began to call: "Oliver Fenton!" cupping his hands so as to shoot the sound straighter and farther before him.

He got no answer out of the wilderness, but he hardly expected one; he simply wanted to send a warning of his coming, so that the hunted father of the girl would not slink away at the noise of footsteps.

At last, breaking into the clearing, he swept it with a

glance, and shouted for the final time, with all his might:
"Oliver Fenton!"

He was silent, then, straining his ear to distinguish an
answer, perhaps far away. Once he thought that he heard a
sound, but he could not be sure whether it was a human voice
coming toward him, or some noise among the trees, for a
wind had risen and was bending them slowly from side to
side.

It was a crossing of his plans and his hopes that he had not
counted on, and he snapped his slender fingers with annoy-
ance. Everything depended upon his ability, he felt, to get to
the spot in time to speak with the fugitive, warn him of the
coming of the sheriff, warn him above all, of the treachery of
Ben Thomas.

And now, having arrived at the proper place, he found that
his quarry was gone. He groaned impotently.

There was nothing for it, however. He drew back among
the trees, found a patch of thick brush, and behind that he
crouched, waiting.

A full half-hour went slowly and wretchedly by. He heard
not a single sound of approach, but suddenly a smallish form
was standing in the clearing where, a moment before, there
had been nothing.

It was Sam Hollis, beyond a doubt. It amused the watcher
as much as it caused him anxiety to watch the prowling
movements of the sheriff.

He admired the way Sam Hollis handled himself. As he
moved, so would Speedy have done under similar circum-
stances, with the same catlike silence, never stepping where
the print of his foot would remain upon the ground or even
upon the cushion of pine needles.

Now he was stooping beside the runlet of water; now he
had broken out a bit of earth from the bank, now he was
washing it in the hollow of his hand.

When he arose, it was with a sudden stiffening of his body,
and Speedy saw that the face of the man had become hard and
cold.

That was what the sight of the gold would always do.
Murder was in the air of that quiet little clearing, into which
the rays of the sun sifted down so pleasantly, and left little

pools and patches and charming embroideries of light upon the ground.

The sheriff drew back and disappeared. There was nothing to see, nothing to hear—only the burbling of the water, and the occasional murmur of the wind.

Then big Oliver Fenton came slowly out into the clearing and looked about him, with a frown.

"Funny doggone thing," he said, aloud. "I kind of thought that somebody was hollering my name around about in here. Some man who—"

His voice trailed away to join his silent thoughts.

Speedy, tiger-keen with eagerness and anxiety, continued a movement that he had begun as soon as the fugitive from justice appeared.

He had hoped, if Fenton came down to the clearing, he might pass close to the spot where he was lying and receive the timely warning. But, in fact, he had come in on the farther side of the clearing, and was closer to the place where the sheriff had disappeared.

So Speedy slid out from the patch of brush, gliding swiftly from the protection of one tree to another. He was almost at the edge of the clearing when the sheriff stepped out from a tree behind Fenton, with a leveled revolver in his hand.

Speedy noted that the gun was held low, hardly more than hip high and thrusting out half the length of the curving arm. That was the way an expert always handled his weapons, in this part of the world.

The sheriff had not spoken a word, had made no move that was audible, when Fenton, as it seemed, became conscious of an unseen danger. With a stifled exclamation, he whirled about, saw the man and the gun and reached for his own weapon.

"Stop!" shouted Speedy.

That unexpected, ringing call out of the woods caused both the sheriff and Fenton to glance to the side.

They saw nothing. Speedy had flattened himself out close to the ground, behind a small, spreading shrub that sheltered him fairly well from view, while it enabled him to peer out at the pair in the clearing.

"I've got you covered, Hollis," said Speedy. "And I'll put

a rifle bullet through the middle of you, if you try to pot him. Fenton, don't be a fool. Keep your hand off your gun. Don't you see that he has the drop on you?''

Oliver Fenton, there was no doubt, would never have submitted to the silent pressure of that leveled gun. He had risked his life too many times in the past three years, to surrender himself to the law without a fight, no matter against what desperate odds.

But now that voice that seemed to come from a friend, stopped him, because it gave him another hope.

"Whoever you be that's layin' up back in there, you're interferin' with the law," said the sheriff. "D' you know that? Or do you think that I'm a holdup artist, maybe?"

"You're Sheriff Sam Hollis and a good man with your hands," said Speedy. "But the point is that you've come for the wrong man."

"I've come for Oliver Fenton, and this is him," said the sheriff.

"Steady, Fenton!" cautioned Speedy, as the big man seemed about to go for a gun again. "Steady, there, partner, and we'll work this out without any gun plays!"

# 10

The sheriff had come, without question, to a full halt, and stood in an utter quandary, while Speedy commanded, briefly: "All right, Fenton. Back up into the woods, will you, and keep going for a while. I'll take care of the sheriff."

Fenton nodded and, stepping back, he found sanctuary within the forest.

"Now, partner," said the sheriff, "what's the end of your play? You've got the drop on me, and I ain't fool enough to play ducks and drakes with a rifle that I can't even see."

"Wait a minute," urged Speedy. "I've got to think it over for a moment."

Even as he spoke, he was drifting away to the left and, once behind the trunk of one of the great pines, he worked rapidly and silently away through the forest gloom, making a swift semicircle that had a radius of a furlong, at least.

Behind him, he heard the sheriff speak again, but, now that he was away from the place, the sheriff, for an instant, was out of his picture and he wanted to see Sam Hollis no more.

What was of a keener interest to him was the shadowy form that, presently, he spotted before him, moving quietly forward among the trees. That was big Oliver Fenton, and coming close up behind, Speedy spoke.

Fenton whirled, with gun ready, hip-high; Speedy raised his hands obediently in the air.

"It's all right, Fenton," said he. "You don't need a gun for me."

A change came in the savage face of Fenton.

"You're the fellow that covered the sheriff," he muttered. "And a good thing for me that you were there, but what brought you? Where's your rifle?"

"My rifle was a bit of bluff. It was dirty work that brought me, Fenton."

"Whose work?"

"That of Ben Thomas."

Fenton scowled. "You've done me a good turn, lad," said he. "Don't be undoing it by running down the truest man on earth!"

His eyes burned as he brought out his confession of faith, but Speedy shook his head.

"Listen to facts, Fenton. I was lying up in a pine tree, yonder, when you and your girl and Thomas were talking together."

"You were what?" exclaimed Fenton.

"You try to believe me. I met the two of 'em at Council Flat, and I didn't like the look of Ben Thomas. It was intuition, if you want to call it that. I talked to him, and my ears liked him even less than my intuition."

"I don't understand what you're driving at," said Fenton, "but man, Ben Thomas has been the best friend and the truest man that ever—"

"That ever cut a friend's throat, eh?" finished off Speedy. "When I heard that they were heading for Trout Lake, I trailed 'em out of the town. I worked up the valley behind them and, when I got their line from the black rocks, I cut ahead and spotted you in the clearing. It was no trick to slide up the back side of a pine tree and lie out on a branch over your head.''

"No trick for a wildcat—I never saw the man that could do it, though," answered Fenton. "But go ahead."

"Why, I saw the evil in the face of Thomas, when he got the gold out of the pan. He looked up, and I looked down, and there was murder in him, plain to see. But you and your girl were too much taken up with one another to watch him. I followed them back to town. I stole the claim papers out of the pocket of Thomas and watched him go down the street and turn in at the office of Sheriff Sam Hollis."

"Ha?" cried Fenton.

His face turned gray as he listened.

"That's what I saw him do," said Speedy, "and any child could have guessed, from that point, why he wanted the sheriff. He had left the girl in the hotel. He'd send the sheriff for you and he'd file the claims in his own name. Consequences could go hang. Is that a clear story?"

"Ben Thomas!" muttered Fenton. "I've bunked with him, ridden herd with him, nursed his children, lent him money, fought his enemies, loved his friends, and now you try to tell me that he's a crook. I won't believe you!"

"Then, why else am I here?" Speedy asked.

"I don't know. You're a demon, for all I can make out."

"It was a gunplay, back there in the clearing," pointed out Speedy. "You were going for your gun, while Hollis had the drop on you, and he's not the man to miss that sort of a shot."

"I'd be on my back, dead," agreed the other. "Yes, and I know it. But what was it that dragged you into this?"

"That doesn't matter," said Speedy. "It's a game that I like. That's all that I can say. But here's another point. When I saw Thomas go into the sheriff's office, I went to the hotel again, persuaded your daughter that Thomas had sent me back there after her because he had to be busy elsewhere, and got her to the bureau to file the claim in her own name alone.''

He shrugged his shoulders, as he added: "I left her waiting in line, while I came up the valley and found you here."

"You did all this for your own pleasure?" demanded the other.

"Never mind why I'm doing it. I've told the yarn for you up to date. How'll you play it from this point on?"

"I'll get to Ben Thomas if I have to walk through fire every step of the way. When I see him, I'll get the truth out of him, or—"

"Or kill him, eh?"

"What else is he fit for but killing?"

"That puts two ropes around your neck," said Speedy. "Listen to me, will you?"

"Of course, I'll listen," said Fenton.

"You're to keep your hands from Ben Thomas. If you meet him, as you're likely to before long, you're to smile in his face. Will you do as I ask?"

"I'd rather tear out his heart."

"And hang for it!" Speedy reminded him.

"I'm to hang for one man already. What's the difference if I hang for two?"

"Because you didn't kill Dodson," said Speedy.

"Ah, didn't I?" muttered the other. "And who was it did kill him, then?"

"Slade Bennett."

"Slade Bennett!" cried Fenton, throwing up one hand before his face, as though a light had blinded him. "Slade Bennett? That scoundrel? Was it him?"

"It was Bennett, I think," said Speedy. "I remember the story of that killing, now. Dodson was a neighbor of yours. There was bad blood between you. He was going downhill, losing money, mortgaged up to the eyes. He'd been drinking and threatening you in a saloon in town. When you heard of that, you saddled your horse and rode away from your place, with your wife and your girl begging you to stay at home. That's the story that was told, at least.

"You came back late that night. The next morning, you were arrested. Dodson had been found dead inside his house, from a knife wound in the throat. The sign of your horse was traced straight up to Dodson's door. Besides, Slade Bennett swore that he'd ridden by, heard voices shouting in the cabin; then a quick silence and the noise of a horse galloping away. That was what made the case against you."

"That was the case," nodded the rancher. "And what makes you think that I didn't kill Dodson, when killing was just what he needed?"

"The look of you tells me that," said Speedy. "You're ready and handy enough with a gun, but you wouldn't use a knife on another man."

"And what makes you think that Slade Bennett did the job?"

"Because Slade would use a knife. He'd used one before! And because he was the man who swears that he heard Dodson name you as the killer. Did Bennett have anything against you before that?"

"Not that I know of."

"He was waiting to see Dodson about something or other," said Speedy. "He listened while you and Dodson had your talk and your quarrel. When you rode away, he stepped in, finished his man, and gave you the credit. That's the story, as I see it."

Fenton, breathing hard, stared for a long moment at the smaller man. "I see it all lined out. And you're right! You're dead right! Slade Bennett did the trick!"

"You can be freed from any crime that you didn't commit," said the boy. "But if you kill Ben Thomas, it's murder, no matter what's the provocation. You have something beside yourself to think about. You have Jessica, eh?"

"What's she to you?" asked Fenton, with a start.

"A fine girl, a straight shooter, and a thoroughbred," said Speedy, calmly, "and nothing else in the world."

"Nothing else?" asked Fenton, narrowing his eyes.

"Nothing else," said Speedy deliberately. "Now, I want to know what you'll do. Will you go to Trout Lake and make a fool of yourself on the trail of Ben Thomas, or will you stay somewhere up here in the woods?"

"I'll stay here," said the fugitive. "That is, I'll stay here if I can. But Hollis will have out a hundred men to comb the woods for me."

"A thousand couldn't find you, if you take to the trees, or to the ground. Stay where I can find you."

Fenton rubbed his knuckles across his forehead.

"Man," he said, "you seem to have me in your pocket. I'd like to know your name."

"I have a lot of names," said the youth. "But a good many people call me Speedy."

"Speedy?" exclaimed the other.

And then he threw back his head and laughed softly.

"I might have guessed, by the wildcat ways of you," said he. "I've heard of you, Speedy. Mostly, I've thought that the yarns they tell about you are just fireside lies. But now I guess they're true."

Speedy brushed his complimentary wonder away, remarking: "If you see Ben Thomas, be friendly with him?"

"I'll do that, if it breaks my heart."

"It won't break your heart. Trust Ben Thomas like a snake in the grass, watch him every second he may be with you, but don't lift a hand!"

Fenton nodded.

"You're gospel for me, Speedy," he said. "But what of Jessica? She's in Trout Lake, with him acting uncle to her!"

"She's with him, but I think that she's in my hands," said Speedy. "Stay here. Don't worry. But keep your eyes open, and we'll find the best way out of this trouble."

# 11

Speedy hurried rapidly down the hillside. When he came to the spot where he had left his horse, he walked more slowly, cast a half circle about the place, like a beast of prey that studies the wind on three sides of a victim before venturing on to the attack. Then he stepped up to the tree where the mustang was tethered.

He had unknotted the reins, when something caused him to stop short. This something was the mark of a heel print, dimly seen on the ground where it had not been trampled over by the restless yellow mustang.

He looked up, with a jerk of his head and stared into the black muzzle of a gun held by Sam Hollis.

"It's you, Speedy, is it?" said the sheriff.

Speedy simply murmured: "Yes, it's I. What's the matter? And who are you?"

"I'm not one of the thousand thugs who'd like to have you where I have you now, Speedy," said the sheriff. "But you know mighty well who I am!"

"I never stood in front of you before in my life," said Speedy.

The sheriff remembered an odd bit that he had heard of this famous man. For it was said that he would not lie, no matter how closely pressed, but fell back upon some slippery prevarication.

He determined to test him, and said, now: "Speedy, answer me, Yes or No. Were you lying up there in the woods, near the clearing where I found Oliver Fenton?"

"You can see for yourself that I've come down from the woods," said Speedy. "What clearing do you mean?"

"Fenton's clearing."

"What Fenton?"

"Oliver Fenton, the man you've just finished talking to back there somewhere. Answer me, Yes or No!"

"Every man has his own way of getting information out of a witness," said Speedy. "Your way is like a good many others that I've listened to. But what do you want with me and who are you?"

The sheriff grinned suddenly.

"You're Speedy, all right," he said.

Then he added: "I kind of thought that there was something about your face that I'd oughta know, when you went by me on the trail. But you sat that mustang so bad, that I couldn't believe it was really Speedy."

"I'm a mighty bad rider," said Speedy.

"You are, if you don't mind me saying so," said the sheriff. "You're a mighty, thumping bad rider. Now tell me what's Fenton to you?"

"What's Fenton to me?" Speedy repeated. "What Fenton?"

The sheriff laughed, but softly. Still, he did not move his gun out of line with the youth.

"It's a lot of information that I'm giving you, I suppose," said he, "if I tell you that I'm Sam Hollis, the sheriff of this doggone wolf-eaten county. I guess it surprises you a lot to hear that?"

"I'm always glad to meet another sheriff," said Speedy.

"Are you?" answered the other. "Speedy, I've got to run you into the lockup."

"I'm mighty sorry for that," said Speedy.

"You've put your hand in between me and my job," said the sheriff. "And I can't have that."

"I don't know what you mean," said Speedy.

"Sure you don't," agreed the other. "You wouldn't be such a fool as to know what I mean. Will you give me your word to ride in, calm and peaceful, to Trout Lake, or do I have to lash you onto the back of that mustang?"

Only for an instant did Speedy hesitate, but in that instant his dark eyes became as coldly shining as black diamonds.

"I'll go into Trout Lake quietly with you, Hollis," he said. "But I'd like to know—"

"The crime you're charged with, eh?"

"Yes."

"Interfering with the law," said the sheriff. "Maybe the charge won't hold in front of a judge, but it'll hold long enough to keep you in jail for a few days, while I'm cleaning up this case. I'm sorry, Speedy. You're not the kind of a man that the law works agin', but duty's duty."

"I know it," said Speedy. "I'll go along with you. I've given you my promise."

It was the sheriff's turn to hesitate a little. Tradition said that the word of Speedy was better than the sworn oaths of any other man. Finally, Sam Hollis decided that he would examine another legend—that Speedy always went unarmed. That was quickly done. He merely had to order those slender hands into the air. Then he patted the clothes of the other dexterously, and located a small pocketknife, only.

"It's true," muttered the sheriff. "Well, then, follow me!"

He led the way down to the trail, where he mounted his horse. Speedy ranged along beside him.

A peculiar warmth of pleasure filled the honest heart of Sam Hollis. He began to look with strong and sudden favor upon his prisoner. He recalled, out of the past, a hundred legends of the great deeds of this man and the work of those incredibly cunning hands. Yet now he was obviously interfering with the clear duty of a sworn officer of the law and he would have to be put aside.

Speedy was saying calmly: "How are things in Trout Lake?"

"How are things in any mining camp," said the sheriff, "in this part of the world? I can't stop the killings. I just manage to keep down the daily average, that's all. The judge doesn't have to work overtime, but the gravediggers do."

"I know," said Speedy. "The fellows all want their fling. I sort of sympathize with 'em, at that. Speaking of gunmen, I thought I saw Slade Bennett in town; just had a glimpse through a window as I was going down the street."

"Yes, he's in town," said the sheriff.

Speedy started a little, the merest trifle, but it was enough to have meaning to the quick eye of the sheriff.

"That was a cast in the dark. You didn't have no idea that Slade Bennett was in town, eh?"

"I know now, though," said Speedy. "I'd expect him at this sort of a show."

"You call him a gunman, eh? I know he has that reputation, but always self-defense."

"Yes, that's his game. It's an old one, too."

The sheriff nodded.

"I've got nothing on Slade Bennett," he said. "Speaking about Fenton—"

"Bennett"—Speedy interrupted, not loudly, but softly, as though unaware that the other had spoken in the interim—"is one of those fellows who practices two hours a day with his guns and his knife."

"Knife?" said the sheriff. "Why d'you say it like that?"

"I hope to tell you, one of these days," said Speedy. "Depending on how long you keep me locked up in the jail."

The sheriff smiled, a wry and twisting smile.

"I know your dodges, Speedy," said he. "Locks and walls ain't made to hold you. But I'll try what a double guard can do with you in an open room, and the lights on twenty-four hours a day.''

Speedy nodded.

"That's a hard combination to beat," he agreed. "After you have me put away, I'd keep my eye on Slade Bennett, if I were you.''

"Thanks," said the sheriff. "I'll take your advice. I'd like to ask you something.''

"About Fenton?" said the boy.

They were coming close to the first shacks of Trout Lake, as they talked.

"About yourself," said the sheriff.

"Every man loves to talk about himself," said Speedy.

The sheriff shrugged his shoulders and then shook his head.

"It's hard to corner you and make you talk, Speedy," said he. "You've made a fool out of me, today, but doggone me, I don't seem able to feel no malice on account of it, and that's a fact.''

"You've got an oversize heart and that's the reason," commented Speedy.

And his eyes met those of the sheriff, gravely, steadily.

The sheriff flushed a little.

"I'll tell you what I'll do," said the sheriff, "if you'll keep out of the way between me and Fenton, and answer one question about yourself, I won't bother you with the lockup.''

"Thanks a lot," said Speedy, "but what's the question?''

"It's this: What do you get out of it? I mean, out of this wandering about, fighting the fights of other men, never cashing in for yourself?''

Speedy squinted at a distant cloud.

"Why do people stretch a tight wire from one tower to another, and then walk across it in a wind?" he asked softly.

The sheriff started.

"I understand," he muttered. "I believe you, too. So long, Speedy. I ought to lock you up. But I've got more instinct than brains in me, and instinct tells me to set you loose. Get on your way!''

# 12

Speedy went straight to the hotel. In the dusty, smoky, crowded little room that served as lobby, he ran into Ben Thomas and the girl. The man glared at him in a rage; Jessica Fenton was pale with anger and silent, while Thomas exploded: "You've come back, have you? After you finished your monkeyshines! You sneak thief! You stole out of my pocket—"

He was in a frenzy of anger. But Speedy lifted one finger and smiled past it in such a singular way that Ben Thomas stopped short.

"I've seen Fenton," said Speedy. "He knows a snake in the grass from an honest man, by this time. Thomas, remember one thing—night and day, I'm watching you!"

He turned on his heel and went out into the street.

He was sorry, in many ways, that he had had to show so much of his hand, face up, on the table, but he was troubled about the girl. There might be enough in what he had said to give her warning.

However, he could not give himself up, for the time being, to this part of the problem. Other things swarmed before him and must be attended to.

He paused at a saloon, pushed through the doors, bought a glass of beer, and sipped half of it.

"I've got a message for big Slade Bennett," he said. "Anybody seen him around here?"

A little smooth-faced man came up, touched his arm, and looked at him out of confiding eyes.

"Across the street, brother," he said softly, and winked.

Speedy did not stay to finish his drink. He turned on his heel and crossed the street into Haggerty's Saloon. It was well into the afternoon by this time and, since the sun was hot outside and the wet sawdust on the floor of Haggerty's

promised coolness within, a score of men were already
leaning their elbows on the bar.

Two men stood out from others, instantly, not because they
were bigger or better than some of the rest, but because the
electric tension of danger had come between them. One was
John Wilson, standing down the bar with his head high, his
face colorless, the lips compressed in a straight line; the
nearer man, his face turned only in profile to Speedy, was
Slade Bennett. The triangular scar that disfigured his cheek
was enough to identify him.

What had happened, Speedy could only guess. But whatever it was—word or gesture or something else—it had
happened just before he entered the saloon. The men along
the bar were beginning to straighten and turn around to watch
the pair.

It was apparent that some vital offense had been given. It
was also patent, from the leaning head and the forward thrust
of the whole body of Slade Bennett, that he had spoken; John
Wilson, crystallized to white ice by the stroke of the thing,
raised his head still higher.

"You can't talk like that to me," he said.

"Oh, can't I?" purred Bennett.

He raised his head, deliberately; he tilted it back, and he
laughed, so that all could see the derision and the confident
scorn in his face.

"What'll keep me from saying it twice over, you're yellow."

It was time for a gunplay, of course, or for a man-sized
punch, at the least.

But John Wilson was still as a stone; lips began to curl as
the men watched. The tension went out of the air. It seemed
perfectly patent that Wilson was going to take water. His eyes
wavered from the sneering gaze of Bennett; Speedy caught
that eye and jerked his head to the side, to indicate the side
exit.

John Wilson, as though hypnotized, turned and made a
long stumbling stride toward freedom.

"Wait a minute!" thundered the voice of Bennett.

Speedy made a step forward, to the elbow of the gunman.

"Don't make a fool of yourself, Slade," said he.

"Who says fool to me?" said Bennett, turning like a tiger.

He looked down from his height into the eyes of Speedy. A big and splendid man was Bennett; and the fury of the bully was fairly throttling him.

With a side glance, he saw that his intended victim had reached the door and gone out through it, and there was no guffaw of laughter for the exit of the coward. Interest had been concentrated upon this new arrival, and his singularly bold speech to so famous a warrior as Slade Bennett.

"You—Speedy—eh?" muttered Bennett, in surprised tones.

His eyes worked an instant as his thought and desire struggled within him. It was only a split part of a second that separated him from the drawing of his gun, but Speedy's mysterious hands were still closer than that.

Still, too much had been contained in that sentence of Speedy; there had to be an accounting or the taking of water would be suddenly shifted to Slade Bennett.

Therefore he demanded, in a harsh voice: "What d'you mean by calling me a fool, Speedy?"

"Calling you a fool? I didn't call you a fool, Slade," said Speedy gently. "I wouldn't do that. I said don't be a fool! There's a good deal of difference, isn't there?"

His smile was so calm, that the other men in the room began to shift their position a little.

Everyone was able to see that this was a man of mark; otherwise, Bennett would have crushed him to the floor and gone after his first victim.

"I don't see much difference," said Bennett, "but I don't mind hearing you try to explain."

"Certainly, I like to explain," said Speedy cheerfully. "It's like this, Slade. You didn't know that that fellow was John Wilson, did you?"

"He might be John Smith, for all I know," said Bennett. "He's yellow, is all that I know about him."

Speedy shook his handsome head.

"Oh, you're wrong, Slade," said he. "You're dead wrong. I'd rather sit in the electric chair than face a John Wilson, when that cold, white look comes over 'em. That's when they kill, and I've never known a man fast enough and straight enough with a gun to hold 'em off. His father was the same way."

"You're joking, Speedy. This is one of your tricks," said Slade Bennett. "Didn't I see the dirty coward sneak out of the place?"

"You saw him go to get a gun," said Speedy, smiling steadily. "That's all you saw him do."

"If he's a man, he'd wear a gun," declared the other.

"Why, he wore a gun too often," said Speedy. "I hear that he's had to swear to his father that he won't wear a gun. He uses it too well, I understand."

"The mischief he does," said Bennett. "If ever I saw a scared kid, he's the one, just now!"

"That's the Wilson look. I don't know how many men before you have gone wrong about it. A lot of 'em, Bennett," said Speedy. "A lot of people have taken the white look of a Wilson for a look of fear. And a lot of people have died, I understand, Bennett. That's why I called out to you when I saw the look on his face. I didn't want you to go wrong. That wouldn't exactly do—seeing that you're an old acquaintance of mine."

"I'm trying to believe you, Speedy," said the other, plainly troubled.

"I know him. I'm a friend of his," said Speedy, confidently. "And I'll try to go and steer him in a new direction, away from you. Otherwise, he'll be back here in a few minutes and the saints help your unlucky soul, Bennett!"

"Is that so?" said Bennett, rearing his head again. "If he's a friend of yours, Speedy, you tell him that right here is where he can find me, and that I stand by what I said."

Speedy sighed. "Well, Slade, I've warned you," he said.

"Cut out the warnings," said Slade Bennett. "Everybody up to the bar."

"Not for me, thanks," answered Speedy, "I'm going to get hold of him and see what I can do. It'll be a hard job, but I'll try my best for you, Slade!"

And he departed, hastily, through the side door of the saloon.

"Who's that?" asked someone of Bennett, who stared at the still swinging door.

"That?" answered Bennett rousing himself from a trance.

"Oh, that's a streak of poison and greased lightning, that's all it is!"

And he turned for his drink.

# 13

Speedy went for the hotel with all the speed that he could make. He felt that his hands were more than filled, because he had a double task before him; the problem of Oliver Fenton was enough; but the problem of John Wilson was equally big and difficult.

When he reached the hotel, he found that Wilson, as he expected, had already gone to his room. He got the number and was instantly at the door, rapping.

After a moment a heavy voice asked who was there.

"Speedy," answered the youth. "I've got to see you. Let me in for half a moment, will you?"

There was no answer.

Speedy, balked by this unexpected opposition, for a moment paced catlike, up and down the hall.

Then he drew a short length of fine steel spring from a pocket and leaned over the lock of the door. Only for a minute or so did he work with this odd tool; then the door fell open before him.

John Wilson had not heard the sound. He lay face down on his bed, his head in his arms and his hands, bent backward, clutching at his hair. Beside him was his revolver; and Speedy, as he closed the door softly behind him, shuddered a little at the sight of the gun.

He knew well what it meant.

Now, shadowlike, he crossed the room, picked up the weapon, and fondled it for a moment. It disappeared presently inside his coat; at the same time, he touched the shoulder of the man, saying: "Well, Wilson, we can talk it over. Will you do that?"

John Wilson came wildly to his feet and glared savagely down at the smaller man. Then he glanced at the closed door.

"How did you get in?" he asked. "That doesn't matter. You can do miracles, everyone says. You can read minds. You can tell fortunes. But you don't have to be a prophet to see that I've ruined my life today! I'm a cur that every man can kick out on the street."

His own agony bent his head far back and silenced him.

"You left the saloon to get a gun," said Speedy. "You come out of a dangerous fighting family. I'm your friend. I knew that you didn't have a gun with you, because you can't trust yourself with one. So I hurried over to the hotel to try to stop you from going back to the saloon and killing Slade Bennett."

The young man stared.

"What are you saying, Speedy?" he demanded.

"I'm telling you the truth."

"And they don't see clearly that I'm a worthless cur?"

"No, they don't see that, because it wouldn't be true."

"I could feel my face was frozen. They saw the white of it. They must have seen that!"

"They saw the Wilson look, that I told them about afterward. The Wilsons all turn white when they're ready to kill."

"You mean to say that they believed you?" murmured Wilson. "They don't think that I'm a coward?"

"Listen to me. Did anybody in the place laugh or taunt you when you left the saloon?"

"No. That's true. I thought they were all too sick, with the feeling of my shame."

"No, they were sure that trouble was in the air, and that you'd left the saloon meaning to come back."

"But I can't go back!"

The face of Speedy puckered a little.

"Not now, perhaps," said he. "But you're going back later on."

"I can't go!" said Wilson. "Look!"

He held out both hands, and Speedy saw that they were trembling. Every nerve seemed to be twitching, making those big, powerful hands as helpless as a child's.

"I'm like that all through," declared Wilson. "I'm shaking all through. I'm hollow inside. I'm not a man. I'm only a rotten shell that looks like the real article.''

He changed his gesture, and suddenly pointed at Speedy.

''You saw straight through me the first time,'' he said.

''I saw that you carried your head so high because you weren't sure of yourself. That was all,'' said Speedy. ''And I saw that you had a lot of strength that you wouldn't trust.''

Wilson sank down on the edge of the bed and held his head in his hands.

''You're wrong,'' said he. ''I'm no good. That's the truth about it.''

''They're waiting for you in the saloon,'' said Speedy. ''Now, you start in and try to pull yourself together, will you?''

''Let them wait!'' groaned Wilson. ''I'm going to sneak out of town while they're still waiting.''

''Very well,'' said Speedy, ''I'll write a note saying that I've managed to stop you for the time being and advising Slade Bennett to get out of town. You understand? I'll send that note over to Haggerty's Saloon. Then I'll come back up here and talk to you again.''

The young man made no answer, and Speedy, with a sigh, hurried from the room.

In the lobby he scribbled:

DEAR SLADE: This devil, Wilson, is still in a white fury. He wants the carving of your heart, and I'm afraid that he'll have it, if you don't give him room. You can slide out of this, and nobody will have it against you. I've persuaded him not to go over at once. That's all I can do. Before long, he's likely to break away from me. And if he gets at you, Slade, he's a dead shot and sure poison.

YOURS, SPEEDY

He folded that paper and shoved it into an envelope. Then he gave it to the rusty-headed boy to carry to the saloon.

''Take that to Haggerty's and give it to Slade Bennett,'' he said. ''There's no answer to wait for. Just put it in his hand, and then slide out.''

He went back up the stairs to the room of John Wilson, to

find that the man had not altered his position. He closed and locked the door.

"Wilson," he said, "you've talked and thought yourself into a panic. You started running, and you ran backwards, instead of ahead. That's all, that's wrong with you. You've still got your chance to fight—to win or go down."

Wilson jerked up his head. A twisted, tormented grin was on his face. His voice was changed, as he said: "I came out here to try to make myself a man. There's nothing inside me that is worth the making, though. Not a thing. I am just a big bluff."

"I don't believe it," said Speedy. "A man can't live as long as you have without being called, sooner or later."

"You don't understand," said John Wilson. "When I was a youngster I was years in one school. Right after I got there, a boy tried me out, challenged me to fight. I had to do it. I stood like a stone, sick. He rushed in at me, I threw out my hand at his head. We clinched, and he lost his footing. We fell, with me on top, and as we dropped, my elbow struck his head. He lay stunned. It was an hour before he came to.

"And all the boys standing around thought that it was my one blow that had knocked him out. From that moment, everybody was afraid of me. None of the boys would fight me, and as long as I was in the school, I was considered a lion. But I knew all the while that I was a coward.

"Then I went to college. A lot of the students from my own school were there before me, and they'd spread the reputation of my terrible strength and my dangerous punch. I wouldn't turn out for any of the athletic teams; only crew. There was no physical competition, no physical contact in that.

"That's my history down to today. Finally, I've been called. And you see what happened. I thought that if I came out here into the wild West, to a rough mining camp, I'd be thrown into a corner, and then I'd have to fight my way out but, when the pinch came, I simply lay down like a yellow coward."

"How did the trouble start between you and Slade Bennett?" asked Speedy.

"I don't know. My mind's a haze. All I can see is the

gloating in his eyes, as I broke down before him. I couldn't even face his eyes, to say nothing of his gun. I came back here to kill myself; and I didn't have the courage for that."

"You've thought about yourself for years," said Speedy. "You've worked up an idea about yourself and the idea's stronger than the fact.

"This is what you're going to do. You're going to wait here till I get word about Bennett. It may be that my bluff has worked, and that he's clearing out. If not, you're going back to the saloon and face him. Here's a knock at the door, now. Maybe that's our answer."

# 14

At the door, when he opened it, Speedy found the rusty-haired boy of the hotel. He had a letter which he shoved into Speedy's hand.

"I dunno what you wrote to Slade Bennett," said the boy, "but it certainly heated him up a lot."

Speedy waved the messenger off and, turning back into the room, he saw the drawn, tense face of John Wilson, staring at him in mingled fear and hope.

It turned the heart of Speedy cold, that fixed, pleading stare. Opening the letter, he found that Slade Bennett had scrawled on the back of the paper that Speedy had sent: "I'm waiting, right here, for another half hour. And then I'm coming over to get the low hound."

There was no signature. The big firm handwriting spoke for itself. Evidently, Slade Bennett saw through Speedy's bluff.

"It's no good," said Speedy. "There's the letter. You've got to go back and face him!"

John Wilson seized the slip of paper and read it over and over. Then he said: "Speedy, I've got to write some letters home, in case anything happens. I'll meet you downstairs. I'd rather be alone for a few minutes. Just leave my gun behind, so's I can look it over before I go down, will you?"

It was a pitifully poor attempt at deception. Suicide was what poor John Wilson meant, and Speedy knew it perfectly well.

But no solution presented itself to his mind. He needed time to think the thing over, time to ponder on it. Besides, it was possible that Wilson really did wish to be alone to write farewell messages.

"I'll leave you alone for a few minutes, Wilson," he said at last. "But then I'll come back and see you. And I'm not leaving the gun behind."

In the outer hall, as he stepped from the room, it seemed to him that he saw a shadow draw back through an open doorway into a room not far from him, the shadow of a tall man.

He hurried to the place.

"Who's there?" he asked, of the empty darkness beyond the open door. A subdued murmur answered him: "Is that you, Speedy?"

He knew that voice. It was not so very long since he had been hearing it. "Fenton!" he said, and glided into the room.

By the glimmering light of the dusk, he saw the big man in a corner; the sheen of a naked gun was in his hand.

"Fenton," said Speedy, "you promised to stay there in the woods. Why did you go and break your word?"

"I didn't give a real promise," muttered the deep, husky voice of the fugitive. "And, the more I thought about Ben Thomas, the more I knew that I had to see him face to face and have a little talk."

"With guns, eh?" said Speedy.

"With guns," said Fenton grimly.

"Nothing's proved against him, so far," said Speedy. "Nothing except my word. Are you going to kill on the word of the first man you hear talk against an old friend?"

"I'm going to find Thomas," said the other. "His room's right down this hallway."

He moved to the door.

"Stop where you are!" said Speedy.

"You can't stop me," said Fenton. "He's in the hotel, and I'm going to get him. If I die for it afterward—well, dying's a small thing to me. There's not much good left in the life that I have in front of me."

Speedy was utterly helpless.

"Fenton," he murmured, stepping closer, "you're a fool. Will you listen while I try to—"

"Listen to me, and stick up your hands, Fenton!" snapped the voice of Sheriff Sam Hollis, just behind him, in the dimness of the hallway!

Fenton, with a groan and a curse, whirled, instead of throwing up his hands. At least, he had not come this far to surrender without a fight. But there was no chance for him against the preparedness of such a fighter as Sheriff Sam Hollis. The gun of the latter barked and, as Speedy sprang forward, the tall body of Fenton toppled back into his arms.

He lowered the weight to the floor.

The sheriff was saying, panting as he spoke: "Had to do it! Speedy, it's you, isn't it? I'm sorry, but I had to."

"The devil take you and what you had to do," answered Speedy bitterly. "You've murdered a better man than you'll ever be!"

"If a killer can be a good man, he may be one," said the sheriff.

"He's not dead," said Speedy, who had been touching the bleeding body with his hands. "He's knocked out, he may be dying, but he's not dead!"

Footfalls were beginning to hurry down the hall in the direction from which they had heard the heavy, booming sound of the gunshot, but the sheriff slammed the door in the face of the curious, as Speedy lighted the lamp that stood on the table in the center of the room.

As the light flooded his face, Fenton opened his eyes.

"I guess that's about all," he said. "I was a fool, Speedy. Just as you said. Get Jessica, will you? I'd like to have her near while I pass in my checks."

Speedy was back on his knees beside the wounded man, tearing away the coat and shirt to lay bare the wound. It was almost exactly above the heart and yet the heart was still beating.

He turned the body over carefully. In the very center of the back the bullet had come out, and around the side was a purple streak, rapidly growing darker.

Speedy gasped with relief.

"You're knocked out, Fenton," he said, "but you're not going to die. The bullet glanced around the ribs. You'll be walking in a week—the sort of a fellow you are."

He raised his head, as he ended, and looked at Sheriff Sam Hollis.

"You have your streaks of luck, too," he said, slowly, and the sheriff, though he understood perfectly what was meant, returned no answer.

They laid Oliver Fenton on the bed. Speedy went to find a doctor, located one in the lobby of the hotel, and waved aside the questions showered upon him by the people in the hallway. Then he went to the room of Jessica Fenton and tapped at the door.

She opened it at once, and at sight of him cried out: "Speedy, I've heard you talking to poor John Wilson. If you drive him back into that saloon, if you tempt him to risk his life, I'll despise you forever!"

"You can despise me to your heart's content," he answered shortly. "But now come with me and take care of your father. Sam Hollis has shot him down. He's not dead; he's only hurt. But he wants you."

Then, as she hurried from the room, he led the way to Fenton, and watched her drop on her knees beside the wounded man.

"Speedy was dead right, Jessica," said her father. "I should have kept away. But I wanted to find that hound of a Ben Thomas—"

Speedy was already in the hallway, speaking to the sheriff; the curious crowd had dispersed when it found that no information about the gun fight was leaking out.

"What'll you do with him, Hollis?" he asked.

"He goes to jail, as soon as he's fit to be carried there," said Hollis. "That's all the news you need from me, and that's about all you get."

"Good," said Speedy. "That's the way for a sheriff to talk. Wash the blood off your hands, and get ready for a new job, Sheriff. You may be needed again, before the evening's over."

He went slowly back to the room of John Wilson, slowly, because the sense of failure was a bitter weight upon his heart. He had failed with Fenton. The man would be tenderly nursed back to life by the men of the law, and then securely hanged by the same careful hands that had tended him in sickness.

That was the end of him. Jessica Fenton would go on through life with the stigma of her father's shameful death on her name. The other problem, John Wilson, well, Wilson would probably never be urged on to toe the mark.

When he opened the door of the room again, he saw that not even the uproar in the hall had drawn the man away from his writing. He was addressing the letter, when Speedy came in. And he winced at the sight of the small man.

Speedy went to the window and sat on the sill. "Ready now?" he asked.

The stone-pale lips of the other made no answer.

"Jessica Fenton can't be wrong," said Speedy. "She and I both can't be wrong about you."

"What does she say of me?" groaned Wilson.

"It isn't what she says about you," said Speedy. "It's the way she looks about you that counts!"


# 15


It's no matter to Speedy how far he carried deception, so long as he could make his point, so long as he could force John Wilson to play the man even for a moment, though he were to die under the bullets of Slade Bennett the next minute.

In fact, Wilson had risen from the table, as one drawn upward by a hand.

"What about Jessica Fenton?" he asked.

"What about her?" echoed the other. "Why, you're not a fool as well as a coward, I hope. You can see what's in a girl's face, when she shows it as openly as Jessica Fenton had showed it to you."

The white face of the young man flushed crimson.

"Maybe I'm both a fool and a coward," said he. "Only, Speedy, has Jessica said anything to you?"

"She didn't write it on paper," said Speedy, "and sign it before a notary. That's the only kind of information that you'd be interested in, though, I suppose."

"I've worshiped her from the day I first laid eyes on her," Wilson said hoarsely. "But I thought—"

"It's all right," said Speedy. "She'll soon be over caring anything about you, when Slade Bennett comes over to kick you out of town!"

The young man closed his eyes and groaned.

And the heart of Speedy sank like a stone in thinnest water. Then a cold demon got him by the throat and made him say: "Go over there and face him, you rat!"

"I can't, I can't," breathed Wilson.

"You can, and you will," said Speedy. "There's your gun. Take it and go over and face him. Throw open the saloon door. Thunder out his name. Ask: 'Where's Slade Bennett?' And then start shooting. You can shoot straight and fast. Every coward learns how to use a gun like an expert."

"It's no good, all my practice," said John Wilson. "There's nothing in me. I can't do a thing; I've got to get out of town; I've got to go."

He started for the door. Speedy stepped in front of him.

"You're not leaving town. You're going with me to Haggerty's Saloon."

"No!" cried Wilson.

"Then, I'll take you!"

"Damn you," gasped Wilson. "Get out of my way!"

And in his frenzy, he struck for the dark head of Speedy, but that lightning-quick eye of Speedy saw clearly enough the coming of the blow. A dozen ways he could have avoided it, but a new thought had come to him and stopped him. There he stood, patient as a log, and let the stroke crash home against his head.

It knocked him flat with a force that skidded him on the floor. A cloud of darkness, mingled with red sparks, flew up across his eyes.

And through that cloud, he saw Wilson leaning above him, and heard the astonished voice gasping: "And that's Speedy!"

Speedy lay still.

"If I can do that to him," muttered the voice of the other, "what's a bully like Slade Bennett to me!"

Suddenly he had snatched the gun from the table on which Speedy had laid it and rushed for the door.

Speedy gathered himself from the floor and followed. His brain was still buzzing but there was triumph in his heart.

There was a hidden courage in big John Wilson. He was hurrying on now to face Bennett. In another thirty seconds, he might lie dead. But from the viewpoint of Speedy, that mattered nothing, or little more than nothing. To die like a man, from his conception, was far better than to live like a coward, haunted forever by fear.

Speedy, running fast, saw the big fellow lurch out of the door of the hotel and crash across the veranda, then race on across the street.

In Wilson, too, there was probably a dread lest the heat of the impulse should cool before it had been given form in action. Speedy was on the heels of the runner, when the latter reached the swinging doors of Haggerty's Saloon and, casting them wide, strode in, shouting: "Where's Slade Bennett?"

As a ripple of water curls around a stone, so Speedy slipped around big John Wilson, and stood some distance along the wall of the saloon.

It was brief. Slade Bennett was standing near the head of the bar and, as Wilson's stentorian shout reached his ears, he wheeled suddenly about, with a deep, muffled cry, the revolver flashing in his hand like the gleam of a knife.

There was even time for Speedy to see Wilson also, as he stood just inside the swinging doors of the saloon, with his head thrown up and back, his face deadly pale.

He had a mere half second to see these things. Then, as big Slade Bennett turned and fired, John Wilson, calmly, deliberately, as it seemed, drew his own gun, and shot Slade Bennett down.

Twice had Slade fired, so much greater was his speed of hand than Wilson's but twice he had missed, and the first fire of Wilson brought down his man.

Speedy went across the floor in an instant, and was on his knees beside the fallen man. He tore open coat and shirt, and found the purple spot out of which the blood was oozing gradually, a mere drop at a time, and, with that glance, and by a look at the purple-white band that was forming around the mouth of Bennett, he knew that the end had come for the gunman.

Slade Bennett did not open his eyes, but in his breathing he groaned and there was a bubbling in his throat.

Other men came up. A hard, ringing voice, just over the head of Speedy, said: "I'm sorry for this. And I'd like to help. What can I do for him?"

Speedy looked up and saw John Wilson, a man transformed. The color was back in his face; his eyes flamed; a sort of transcendent power was quivering in his voice.

And Speedy said coldly: "The thing for you to do, and all the rest, is to take off your hats. Slade Bennett's dying. Where's a doctor?"

There was always at least one doctor present in such a crowd, in those days, and now the man of science came forward to do what he could.

But Speedy did not leave the fallen man.

He said: "Slade, Slade! They've found out about everything. They've found out that you murdered Dodson. What are we going to do about it?"

The eyes of Slade Bennett flashed open and closed again; his mouth sneered.

"Dodson had to get it," he said. "You know why I killed him, Jerry. After I stabbed him, I made it look as though that fool, that Oliver Fenton, had turned the trick. The sheriffs have been hunting Fenton, and I've walked about the streets. Jerry, open the window, open the door, I'm choking!"

He raised himself on his hands with his eyes wide, but unseeing.

On his hands and his heels his body stiffened an instant; then he collapsed.

Speedy, reaching past the doctor, closed the eyelids as faithfully as if he were that "Jerry" for whom his voice had been mistaken.

Slade Bennett lay dead on the floor, and the men who had gathered close for an instant to look down into the dead face were now scattering to find their drinks in another saloon.

And Speedy heard a voice that said: "Wilson, that was the

coolest trick and the best gunplay that I ever seen. I wish that you'd come and have a drink with me. My name's Thompson.''

Speedy listened to the voices depart; for his own part, he remained fixed and still beside the dead man, feeling once again, as he had so often felt in the past, that something out of his own bright spirit had fallen and lay like a dissolving shadow there, before his own eyes.

# 16

Then, in the saloon across the street, he found John Wilson celebrating in the midst of a circle of newfound friends.

He touched the arm of the young man and, looking up, he saw Wilson turn and look down at him with eyes of liquid fire. The icy barrier of half a lifetime of restraint and discontent had fallen.

But when he saw Speedy, he stepped through the crowd at the bar and laid his hand on the shoulder of the smaller man.

"I know part of what you've done for me, Speedy," he said. "I can guess at the rest. You let me hit you, back there in the hotel room. Speedy, is that right?"

Speedy made a brief gesture to disclaim the suggestion. Then he muttered: "Wilson, you've done part of the great job. Now go over and collect on it."

"Collect on what?" asked Wilson.

"On the killing of Slade Bennett."

"I've got an idea," said Wilson, suddenly frowning, "that I never could have done anything with him, except that the bluff that you'd put up for me unnerved him a little, when he heard me rush into the saloon and bawl out the words that you wanted me to shout. There's nothing for me to collect out of the killing of Slade Bennett, except a chance to pay his funeral expenses, and I'm glad to do that."

Speedy nodded rather grimly, as he surveyed the other.

"You're a good fellow, Wilson," said he. "And I'm mighty glad of that. But I'll tell you what you're to collect. That's the girl—Jessica Fenton. Come down with me to the jail this moment—no, they won't have moved Fenton, yet. He'll still be in the hotel. And we'll go and take Fenton away from the sheriff."

Wilson frowned.

"I don't know what you mean, Speedy," said he. "If the law—"

"The law has nothing to do with Oliver Fenton," said Speedy. "Slade Bennett has barely finished confessing that he killed Dodson. That's enough to suit the law. Oliver Fenton is free, and you can stand in on the party as the hero of the hour."

"You're laughing at me," said Wilson gloomily.

"I'm not laughing," answered Speedy. "I mean what I say. Now, you come along with me."

He took the big hand of Wilson and drew him out of the saloon.

As they came under the open stars, in the fresh air of the night, Wilson halted suddenly.

"Speedy," he said, "I seem to be seeing the face of the world for the first time. And I've you to thank for that and I do thank you. Will you believe me?"

"Of course, I'll believe you," said Speedy.

"You let me manhandle you, just to raise my spirits, and get me started?"

"Nonsense," said Speedy, carelessly. "I don't let people manhandle me, if I can help it, as a rule. Come on, man, come on. Jessica Fenton's up there. She's the one that would like to hear from you."

"Did you know," said John Wilson, still immovable in the street, "that I confessed everything to her about—about what I've been in the past?"

"No," said Speedy.

"I did, though," answered Wilson. "And she told me that she had faith in me. You know what she based her faith on?"

"What?" murmured Speedy.

"On what you'd said to me back there in the station house at Council Flat—that there was the fear of danger in me, but that I was stronger than I thought."

"You've talked enough," said Speedy, not unpleasantly. "Now go up there in the hotel. Step along. See Jessica

Fenton, and talk to her. You've started in the right direction tonight, man, but you'll need a woman like that to keep you there!''

John Wilson, with a start, straightened and then hurried across the street. Speedy followed more slowly, and came into the lobby of the hotel a sufficient distance behind the new-made hero to appreciate the silence that came over the buzzing room as Wilson entered.

All eyes were turned toward the stairs up which Wilson had disappeared at a run, and Speedy followed, smiling faintly. It seemed that there was little more for him to do, in this case, except to look on at the fruition of his work.

He got to the upper hall in time to see Wilson knock at the door of the room in which the wounded man was lying. The door opened; and he heard the outcry of a happy girl's voice. Well, the news had come before him to the hotel, and the Fentons knew that Oliver Fenton was free!

Speedy nodded and sighed.

He stepped closer. Voices boiled up within the room like water in a teakettle. The door opened again, and the sheriff came out, with a wide grin on his face.

Speedy was near enough to hear, as the door closed, the voice of big John Wilson, saying: ''It's nothing, Jessica. I didn't come here to be thanked. I only came here to say that for your sake, I wish that I could have faced down a dozen like Slade Bennett. And—''

The sheriff laid his hand on the arm of Speedy.

''There it goes, Speedy,'' said Sam Hollis. ''You've spoke some hard words to me, lately, but I'm ready to forget 'em. Now that Fenton has turned out innocent, and Slade Bennett was the guilty man, why, it looks as though I was pretty mean to Fenton. But I had nothing against him; it was only the law, not me, that wanted him.''

''Where's Ben Thomas?'' asked Speedy.

''Ben Thomas won't be seen around these parts for quite a spell,'' said the sheriff soberly. ''He showed up to ask his share of the blood money, when he heard that Fenton was caught, and I told him that he could have all the blood money, when it was paid, and in the meantime, he could have my opinion of him. When I got through talking—and I talked in front of the whole crowd—he sneaked out. There was some talk of tar and feathers, but I guess all that the boys did was to give him a mighty fast ride out of town.''

"It would be a lot better for him if he had had a bullet through the brain,'' said Speedy. "When I first saw him with the girl, I smelled blood as surely as any hunry cat, Sheriff; but he's still breathing, yet he'll never be able to look a decent man in the face from now on. And the blood I smelled was Slade Bennett's!''

"Yes,'' said Sam Hollis. "Heaven help him, and every other man that lives by knife and gun, like me, Speedy, or like you, though the only tools you use are your bare hands. Come and have a drink with me, will you?''

"Yes, a drink is what I need,'' said Speedy. "But wait a minute.''

He paused, raising his hand in the dimness of the hall, and canting his head to listen.

"Aye,'' said the sheriff, "they're all contented enough now. There was a rope around the neck of Fenton, ten minutes or so ago; and the girl was breaking her heart for him; and John Wilson was thought to be a yellow-livered coward. And now listen to the three of 'em laughing together!''

"They're laughing,'' said Speedy, as he moved down the hall again, hooking his arm through the sheriff's. "I only hope that they're not laughing too soon.''

"Now, whacha mean by that?'' asked Sam Hollis.

"Nothing, nothing,'' said Speedy, hurriedly. "Let's get to that drink.''

# Part Two

# 17

Jessica had been looking for Speedy for a month. No one had even admitted having heard of him until she had ridden down a ravine and found the tramp jungle and old Alkali Pete. He had sent her to San Lorenzo. A scar-faced, guitar-playing peon at the hotel there might take her to Speedy, or he might not.

This was the hotel to which Jessica Fenton Wilson went, as soon as she got off the train. She carried with her a roll not of blankets, but of luggage, and a small roll it was, too, for that brown-faced girl knew as well as any man how to travel across country with no more than salt, matches, and a rifle by way of provisions.

When she came to the hotel, the clerk smiled at her, found his smile freezing, and finally assigned a room to her. She went up and found it was at the rear of the hotel, in the least desirable part of the building. However, it had a good big window sunk through the enormous depth of the wall, and in addition there was an immensely deep and comfortable bed.

It was just before noon, and she was starving, so she went down as soon as she had washed her face and hands, and got a little round table under one of the huge trees.

The river ran almost at her feet, bubbling and rippling, the current setting well in toward the bank at this point. Round about under the trees there was a ragged effect of lawn, thriving where the trees shadowed it, scorched where the sun struck it in the middle of the day.

She ordered beans, hot beans—the hotter the better. She had tortillas, big and moist, delicious beyond all other food to the palate that has learned to appreciate Indian corn. She had roast kid, that had been turned on a spit and thoroughly browned. When she finished her meal and her coffee, she felt that she never had dined more heartily or better in her life.

All through the meal, she was looking curiously about her for that small Mexican, that peon whose face was deformed by a scar—that lad who alone in the world could tell her where Speedy was to be found!

It was not until she had finished her coffee that the entertainment began. It was not a whole orchestra—for the midday meal that would have been an extravagance—but a single singer, who thrummed a guitar and sang a song of old Mexico in a soft, pleasant voice.

She could not see him, for the moment, and she dared not start up to go looking for him. The last warning of the old tramp had been that she was not to mention aloud the name of the man she was hunting for. She must exercise the greatest caution.

The singer came nearer. Presently, he was only on the other side of a vast cypress. She heard a husky-throated Mexican growl out a demand for another song of another sort. The song followed.

And very well delivered it was. He sang with verve and with fire; she could fairly see him throw back his head and pour forth his spirit in song.

The singing ended.

"Catch this," said the Mexican.

There was a light *spat*, as though a heavy coin had landed in the flat of a palm.

Then Juan came into view around the trunk of the tree.

His face might have been quite handsome, poor lad, except that it was puckered and twisted by the grip of a big scar that deformed him. Nevertheless, he was not hideous. There was wistfulness in the puckering lines of his forehead and eagerness in his fine, dark eyes.

His skin was very dark, almost blackish-brown. His legs were bare and the sinewy feet were slipped into cheap sandals. The guitar, as Alkali Pete had said, was suspended about his neck by a thick leather strap.

Juan, as he saw the girl, greeted her by taking off his big, cup-shaped straw hat and making a bow which showed her the back of his head and lean, athletic shoulders.

Would she hear a song? She would. What would she have? Why, anything that his fancy selected.

Instantly he was at it. She hardly heard the music, or listened to the romantic words of the ballad, for she was hastily scratching words in Spanish on a bit of paper, that asked: "Do you know Speedy? Can you bring me to him? Or bring him to me? I would give you a fine reward."

As he finished the song, she smiled and held out a twenty-five-cent piece. Along with it she dropped into his hand the wadded ball of paper.

That was discreet enough, surely, but how dexterous was the young man in closing his fingers over that paper ball, without the slightest hesitation!

He went off; he sang again; and she, in the meantime, leaned back in her chair with her eyes closed, feeling that she was about to faint. Juan could bring her to Speedy, if only the youth pleased to do so. Would he please? She should have given him more than a quarter. He would be disgusted and he would not trust her for the reward that she promised in the note.

She grew so sick at heart, thinking of this, that she went from the garden straight up to her room, and there she lay on the bed with her eyes closed, besieged by wretchedness until sleep came to her at last.

When she awakened, the room was dark, and there was a light, scratching sound at the window.

"Don't be afraid," said a voice in Spanish. "It is Juan, señora."

She leaped from the bed and lighted the lamp. Her thoughts were spinning dizzily. It seemed to her that the scarred face of the youth, as he stood in the corner of the room, drifted this way and that before her eyes.

How had he come? The door was locked still; the wall beneath the window was a sheer drop of two stories to the ground.

"You have asked for Speedy," said Juan.

"Yes, I heard that you could take me to him, Juan," said

Jessica Wilson. "I have plenty of money to make it worth while. Are you sure that you can really take me to him?"

"Oh, yes," said the youth, and a painfully twisted smile came on his face.

Then he added: "But who told you that I know him?"

"It was a tramp, a big fellow with a cropped gray head of hair."

"Alkali Pete?" he asked.

"Yes."

"He talks, then?" asked Juan gloomily.

"I had a very hard time dragging it out of him. He's not a gossip, Juan. But about Speedy, when do you think that I can see him?"

"Why, señora—now, if you please."

"Oh!" she exclaimed. "Take me to him instantly, Juan! I think he'll reward you, too, for being my friend."

A strange voice, pitched deeper, said to her: "Don't you know me, Jessica?"

She stared, bewildered. For the voice came from the youth.

"Know you?" she gasped.

"I can't take off the scar; I don't dare wash off the stain, Jessica," said he. "But I thought that an old friend like you might know me again at the first glance."

"Speedy!" she cried, and ran to him with her hands flung out.

# 18

Even in that moment of her emotion, she could not help noticing how deftly and surely he caught her two hands with his, with no uncertainty of gesture.

"It's been a month, Speedy," she told him breathlessly. "I've hunted half the world over, it seems to me. I still don't believe that it's you beneath that scarred face!"

"You know that a little plaster and a little dye will do a lot to a face," said Speedy. "Speak softly. These walls are thick, but there are some ears not far away that I don't want to hear the name of Speedy. Your husband's giving you trouble. What kind?''

"How did you know that he's giving me trouble?'' she asked, half offended.

"Nothing else would make you hunt a month to find me,'' said Speedy. "Nothing but John and his welfare. Tell me about it.''

"He's gone absolutely wild,'' said the girl. "That's the only way to put it.''

"He's gone wild?'' murmured Speedy.

She had rehearsed the speech a hundred times; she knew exactly what she intended to say to him; but now the words evaporated. She simply stuttered: "He's left me, Speedy. That's all. And he'll never come back to me, I'm afraid.''

He considered what she had said gravely. "John was willing to die for you,'' he said, at last. "I suppose that he's just as fond of you, still. You have everything to give him, too. You have a good ranch that your father fixed up for you. And John likes the Western life. So what went wrong?''

She tried to find the right words again, and then an inspiration came to her.

"Would you be happy, leading a life like that?'' she asked.

He shrugged his shoulders. "We're talking about John, not about me.''

"Be honest, Speedy,'' she pleaded.

"No,'' said he, at last. "No, I don't suppose that I'd be happy.''

"Then tell me why.''

"A ship isn't happy when it's always lying at anchor.''

"I don't follow that.''

He explained: "Well, I take it that some men are made for movement, and others are made to stay still and work in one spot. I suppose that I'd be contented to stay in one place, if enough things were always happening.''

She nodded at this. "That's the only way I can explain John and what he's done,'' she replied.

"Go on,'' he urged. "He simply left you, one day?''

"He told me,'' said the girl, "that he couldn't be contented as long as the money that had bought the ranch came from father. He said that he wanted to go out and make his share, and prove that he was a man. Then he'd come back. Perhaps that's how he really convinced himself, honestly. But I know that other things were lying behind it.''

"Such as what?''

"He'd lived a pretty sheltered, quiet life, before he came west, but that day when he fought with Slade Bennett and killed him—after that day, John was changed. You know how changed he was.''

"He'd found his self-confidence, that's all,'' said Speedy.

"Something more than that,'' she answered. "After that day, he found that everything in life was dull, except the thing that you love also.''

"What's that?''

"Danger,'' said the girl.

Speedy moved a little farther back from her. "What do you mean by that?'' he demanded brusquely.

"It's the truth,'' she insisted. "Nothing matters to you, Speedy, except danger. That's the explanation of why you drift about the world with a hundred names and a hundred disguises. If you let yourself be known, everyone would be afraid of you, and danger would run away from you. And that's what you want to avoid.

"Why won't you carry a gun? Because that would make a fight too safe a thing for you. Oh, I realize what's in your mind. And now you've come to such a point that nothing pleases you, nothing excites you, except to be in a room with a half-mad gunman, he with a gun, and you with your bare hands!''

"You'd make me out a monster,'' he protested.

"Answer me frankly, Speedy. Isn't it true?''

Instead of answering, he sighed, and looked down for a moment toward the floor. Then he looked up. Even now, his answer was an oblique one.

"You think that John has caught that sort of a fever?'' he asked gravely.

"I don't think so. I know it,'' said the girl.

Speedy shook his head and sighed again.

"Any signs when he was back at the ranch?'' he asked.

"Not many. He was keeping himself in hand. Then there was the novelty of being married, I suppose. Besides that, he was busy working on the ranch, learning the ways of the range. But gradually, I noticed that he was growing absent-minded at the table. He dropped into the habit of taking rides through the night, also. It's a wild country up there, you know.''

"I know," said Speedy gently, almost tenderly.

The girl continued: "We had some pretty wild horses. There were seven or eight bad ones that father had picked up for a song and turned over to us; they came cheap because they were outlaws, and it was just one of father's rough jokes. But John took them seriously. He settled down to breaking those horses. He was smashed and battered to bits nearly every day. I don't know why he wasn't savaged.''

"Because a horse knows when the rider isn't afraid," put in Speedy quietly.

"Perhaps that was it," she admitted. "At any rate, he worked for a month. And all that month he was happy, laughing and singing about the place. At the end of two weeks, he rode one of those outlaws to a standstill. Thirty days after the start, he had every one of the lot in hand.

"Then the horse breaking ended, and I thanked heaven for it. But, after a few days, I almost wished that he were back at the work again, because his spirits were low every day, and he began that dreadful night-riding again.

"In the middle of this, we missed some cows. They'd been rustled. We located the trail and the pass through the hills that they'd been driven through, and John took three men and went off after them.

"Three days later, the other men came back. I'll never forget the sickness in my heart when I looked out the window and saw them coming, without John. But it turned out that they simply couldn't stay with him.

"A week later, he came back and he drove the cattle ahead of him. There was a bandaged man riding before him, herded along among the cows. That was one of the rustlers. The other rustler—there had been two, you see—would never ride again. He was dead. John had killed him, as he killed Slade Bennett—as he'll kill other men, until one day he's overmatched, or beaten by luck and is shot down and killed! Oh, Speedy,'' she ended, with a high-pitched cry of grief, "I know that he's like you. He caught the fever from you, and there's nothing in the world that will ever content him, except to fight, to fight against odds!''

Speedy went to her and separated the tense hands which she had gripped tightly together.

"Well," he said softly, "after that affair of the cattle rustlers, what happened? He sat about the house, growing more and more absentminded again."

Tears were still streaking down the face of the girl; but she nodded in agreement.

"It was the same way," she said, "until one night he woke me up and stood by my bed, dressed for the road, with his hat in his hand, and a pack on his shoulders. He said that he was leaving the place, for a while, and that he'd stay away until he was able to make a stake and not live the rest of his days on my father's charity."

"Did you say that there was a pack on his back?"

"Yes. He wouldn't even take a horse from the place. He said that everything belonged to me, and from that time on he'd earn everything that he wore or ate or rode or used in any way."

"Did you beg him to stay?" asked Speedy.

"No," said the girl. "I just went down to the front door with him and tried to keep smiling. I told him that what was best for him would have to be best for me, too."

She put her hands over her face and shuddered, remembering that moment.

"You're the wisest girl that I ever knew," said Speedy.

She snatched down her hands and stared at him. "And now, Speedy?" she breathed. "Will you help me?"

"You want me to find him and take him home?" he asked slowly.

"It isn't the finding him," answered Jessica Wilson. "I know where he is. And it isn't merely to bring him home. Oh, he's been back once or twice, just to drop in on me. He's written about his plans. He's always about to strike it lucky and come back for good. But I know in my heart that there's no lucky strike in the world so big that it will satisfy him. It isn't gold he wants, but danger! And who can cure him, Speedy, except the man who gave him the disease?"

She came closer to him, as though that would make him feel more the force of her pleading.

"You want me to change his heart, Jessica. Is that it?" he asked.

"I want a miracle, Speedy," she confessed. "I'm sorry. I know that even you can't do it, probably. But I'm standing here and begging you to try. Will you?"

"I'll try," said he. "You'll tell me where he is. Yet, there's a little job that I'm trying to do here in San Lorenzo. Do you mind if I take a few days for that, before I start on the trail? I've almost run one quarry to the ground, and—"

"Speedy, it's blood out of my heart, every minute you wait."

"Then I'll go," he answered instantly. "I'll start the moment you tell me where to find him."

# 19

When Speedy looked out through the door into the long, low room, he saw twenty men or more seated around the table. The cook had told him to go in and sit down with the rest of the logging crew. There were, in fact, extra places laid, and there seemed to be plenty of food left on the great platters, in spite of the heaps of beans, pale, soggy, boiled potatoes, and half-fried bacon that were constantly transferred to the plates.

The first glance at the crowd showed Speedy all these details of the picture; the second glance showed him John Wilson. He sat near the farther end of the table, talking and laughing with the men around him, a glowing spot of good cheer in the rather gloomy assemblage. For that camp was well above the frost line, and the bitterly cold air seeped in through the cracks of the door and the two windows.

At the end of the table nearest the door sat the boss, distinguished by a clean shirt and a felt hat pushed to the back of his head. Speedy paused by him.

"The doctor told me that I could sit in," said he.

The boss turned a burly face, and surveyed Speedy with a glance that had in it neither surprise nor interest; only his eyes seemed to hold some contempt for the size of this man, as he pointed toward an empty place with the heel of his table knife.

Speedy sat down. He was a good middle height, but he was dwarfed among these fellows. Mountain lumbermen are the biggest of the mountain breed. It requires a certain span of shoulders to swing an ax to the best effect.

However, there was a certain degree of hospitality shown by those nearest him. One large, grimy hand dragged a platter of beans nearer to him; another shoved forward a basin stacked with hot corn bread. He helped himself, with thanks, and began to eat, without so much as turning his head up or down the table. Too much curiosity is not expected of guests in the West.

At the same time, for all his apparently diligent attention to his plate and to nothing else, every face and form were imprinted on his mind and he weighed every man at the board with lightning glances.

So, very quickly, he made sure that he had seen none of these men before, not one, except John Wilson.

Keen as his memory was, he would hardly have remembered that man, except that he expected from the words of Jessica Wilson to find her husband here.

For Wilson looked older; he was thin and brown of face, now, and looked heavier and harder about the shoulders. Among all these mountaineer giants, he was dwarfed by none. A casual eye, even a most judicious one, might well have selected him as the best hand of the lot—not for sheer size, perhaps, but for the strength of spirit that shone out of his eyes. He seemed in the highest degree pleased with this world in which he found himself. Speedy could not help realizing that John Wilson was no longer what he had been at Council Flat, or again in the mining town. He was more. He was much more. He had nerve to match his bulk.

The source of his good nature began to appear presently, as the clatter of knives and forks grew less, and the men fell back upon their last cups of coffee. In this comparative silence, the voices at the farther end of the table could be heard more clearly, and it was plain that John Wilson, whatever he had been doing before was now badgering a Canuck who sat across from him. The man soon reached the limits of his patience. With a yell of rage he hurled his coffee cup across the table, half filled with the scalding liquid, and followed the cup with a leap at the throat of John Wilson.

Up rose John Wilson, with the gleam of a knife driving toward his own throat. But, as he rose, his updarting hand struck the right arm of the Canuck to the side. With his other hand, he took him by the throat, and he drew the burly man straight across the top of that massive table, which shuddered from end to end.

Metal plates, cups, forks, knives, platters, crashed on the floor, hurled by the kicking legs of the Canuck. But that was not what interested Speedy. He paid a little attention to the expert handwork of John Wilson. But he paid still closer interest to the face of the young man. Perfect and shining bliss was in the eyes of Wilson. It only brightened, as he avoided the second murderous upthrust of the knife.

It glowed to a fire as, at last, he struck the Canadian senseless with a well-aimed stroke of the fist.

The boss came charging up.

"Throw that cursed knife artist out of the camp!" he roared. "Kick him out, and throw his pack after him. If I catch him here in the morning, I'll hang him to the first tree. Shorty, make out his time and pay him off, hear me?"

"Yeah, I hear you," said Shorty.

"And now for you!" continued the boss.

He whirled on his heel, and faced big John Wilson. "I'm through with you. It ain't the first time that you've started pandemonium popping around here. You've picked out three of the best men I've got, and you've had a fight with every one of 'em. You don't know one end of an ax from another. I'll have no more of you. I'm gonna throw you out!"

"Throw me out?" asked John Wilson.

"I'll throw you out, if I gotta have guns to do it," shouted the maddened boss.

"Well, let's see," said Wilson.

He stepped a little forward, and ran his eyes over the crowd of men.

"Guns or no guns," said John Wilson, "you won't throw me out of your camp, Weatherby. You haven't enough men to do it, and they're not the right kind!"

A shout of anger broke from several throats, and now Speedy leaned forward, in the intensity of his interest. His own eyes glowed yellow as the eyes of a hunting lion. And he saw the same light in the eyes of John Wilson, as the man faced these enemies.

They were ready to rush him, yet he stood his ground and taunted them. But that right hand which was draped so carelessly upon his hip, did not intend to occupy itself with either fist blows or a knife handle. Something better than that was surely in its reach.

# 20

It might be that John Wilson was armed, but, no doubt, there were other guns in that rough crowd, though they were not drawn. Speedy could tell the reason. It was simply because the man so openly asked for trouble that he did not get it.

The boss showed himself a man of sense, for he called out, suddenly: "There'll be no blood on this here floor; nobody go near that ruffian! Wilson, you might've showed more sense than this."

"I'm ready to be fired, chief," said John Wilson. "I simply don't want to be thrown out. It's a cold night, and I don't want to be marched out into it."

"Then stay in the bunkhouse tonight," said the boss. "I'm not gonna have gunfighting around here. And I'll tell you this, Wilson, one of these days you're gonna find yourself in a jail or else hanging from a rope collar off the branch of a tree. And I don't care much which thing happens to you. Shorty, make out Wilson's time, will you?"

"Never was gladder to make out anybody's time since I came here," said Shorty with a snarl. "You're a bully, Wilson, and every bully gets his, in the long run."

"That may be," said Wilson, shrugging his heavy shoulders. "I'll go and sleep on that, and I'll leave you boys tomorrow morning. So long!"

He waved his hand at them and strode toward the door.

Sullenly they gave way before him. One man made a move as though to throw himself at the back of the big fellow, but he was held by a companion.

"Gun plays are no good," said the lumberjack with the restraining hands. "We ain't gonna start anything like that here!"

More talk was following, as Speedy slipped from the crowd through the door and stepped into the open night.

It was cold and crystal clear. The sweetness of the air, after the smoky, steaming atmosphere of the bunkhouse, sank to the bottom of his lungs at every breath, and so for a moment he forgot the purpose for which he had made this journey, forgot Jessica Wilson and her husband, and lost himself in the tingling beauty of the mountain night.

A shudder of increasing cold went through him. Then he stepped on and pushed open the door of the bunkhouse. It was built long and low, like the dining room, but larger. There was a stove toward either end, each reddening with the fire that burned in it. But even that double source of heat hardly expelled the chill from the room. It was lighted, similarly, by two smoky lanterns that filled the place with dim shadows.

Wilson, when the door was thrust open, was halfway down the room, arranging the blankets of his bunk, and he turned like a flash, as though to face danger. Speedy walked straight toward him, and saw the frown of Wilson turn into curious wonder. Then a cry came from the lips of the big man.

"Speedy!"

He ran to meet him; and Speedy smiled and waved his hand in greeting, before he gripped the big fingers of his friend.

"Speedy, where did you drop from?"

"Out of the sky, where all good people come from," said Speedy. "I've just been watching you jam things up in the dining room."

"I guess I made a fool of myself," said John Wilson, frowning. "You know, Speedy, I got some smoke in the brain, sort of—"

He paused a moment, entangled in his words.

"You got fire in the brain, and that's different," answered Speedy.

"Fire?" repeated Wilson.

"Who wants to live like a log?" asked Speedy, rather sharply. "I don't, for one, and I'm glad to see that you don't, either, John."

"You take it that way?" asked Wilson.

"Of course, I do. That was worth while—to stand up there and tell the lot of 'em to go to the Old Boy."

"Well, I'm relieved that you take it that way, Speedy," said John Wilson. "But, then, I might have known that you would! That's why you drift around. Trying to find something worth mixing with. But what brought you up here, Speedy? You didn't see Jessica, did you?"

"Jessica?" said the other. "Look here, John, why should I see Jessica?"

"I didn't know. Only, you see, Speedy, I'm trying to make a decent stake for myself. Tired of living on her father's charity. That's what it amounted to!"

"You're right," said Speedy cheerfully. "I don't blame you. You cut loose, did you, to make your own pile?"

"That's it," answered Wilson.

"Perhaps," said Speedy, "if you're really on the loose, we can travel together for a while!"

Wilson exclaimed loudly with pleasure. "Son," he said, "there's nothing in the world that I'd like so well. Will you go on with me tomorrow morning?"

"I can't wait that long," said Speedy. "Sorry, but I've got to stir my stumps."

"Hold on! Start out in the middle of a cold night like this?"

"It's not very cold," said Speedy. "I've seen nights a lot worse. Oh, you might get a nip of frost in a foot or a hand, but that's nothing."

John Wilson cleared his throat and then sighed.

"Well, Speedy," he said, less enthusiastically, "I'm with you, if you say the word. We'll start now."

"Roll your blankets, then. Have you got a horse?"

"Yes, I've got a horse picketed out in the field behind the stable."

"Saddle it up, then. I'll be ready in ten minutes, and meet you in front of the cookhouse. Is that a go?"

"Only, Speedy, what's the terrible rush and the night's like ice!"

"It's a long story, old man," said Speedy. "But the chief thing is that if I don't keep lively on this trail, I'm likely to be dead on it. You understand?"

"You're followed?"

"Yes."

"By whom?"

"Later on I'll tell you. Are you starting with me? Mind you, John, if you ride with me, the way may be a little rough. But if it's excitement you want—"

"I'll meet you in front of the cookhouse in ten minutes," said Wilson curtly.

Speedy stepped out again into the night.

# 21

All was by no means clear in the mind of Speedy at this time. His scheme was still a vague one. The hunger for danger, was what now possessed the very soul of Wilson. It was, therefore, Speedy's task to eradicate that appetite. How he would go about the business, he did not know. But he saw the need of it.

What the foreman of the lumber camp had told John Wilson was undoubtedly true. He would either end with a rope around his neck and his feet dancing on thin air, or else he would find himself in jail. A man cannot hunt trouble, west of the Mississippi, without eventually finding more than he can digest. Furthermore, John Wilson carried a gun, and knew only too well how to use it.

Speedy shook his head, as he reached the gloom of the stable, and began to saddle his mustang. Much trouble might lie before him. It was, in fact, only through danger of the most breathtaking kind that he could hope possibly to cure his friend, as it seemed to him, and send him back to poor Jessica Wilson prepared to settle down to life on a ranch.

But to the swift mind of Speedy the plan came, even while he was pulling up the cinches.

What he conceived was enough to make even his own steady nerves jump. Part would be fact and part would be fancy, in what he said to his companion. But already he was composing the speech when he rode the mustang out under the light of the stars and joined big John Wilson in front of the dining cabin.

He had not even had a goal for this midnight journey, in the beginning. He had merely felt that, from the first, it would be well to make the days which Wilson spent with him as arduous as possible. For himself, he could sleep in the saddle, closing one eye at a time, as it were. Or he could lie down on a bare rock, relaxing utterly for an hour, and then rise refreshed. Heat, cold, thirst, hunger, he had endured so many times that they were his familiars. It would be very strange if Wilson, in spite of his bulk and muscle, could endure the same strains. He must be worn down. When the crisis came, it must be intense enough fairly to overstrain every nerve.

There was another and a grimmer side of the question. Once entered through the door of this adventure which Speedy had conceived, could they escape with their lives?

That question he could not answer. He dismissed it, finally, with a shrug of his shoulders.

In the meantime, they were riding farther up the pass, the horses stumbling in the deep ruts which the logging carts had dug into the ground.

A moon had joined the stars, and the light which it poured down through the pass was like a ghostly spray. They were cold to the bone. John Wilson was shuddering with the bitter weather. But he made no complaint, merely thrusting forward his head in a way that did not entirely please Speedy. He would have been more at ease if he had only seen signs of weakness in his friend!

They reached the height of the pass. Before them extended a broken country of rough mountains, ragged ravines, and a mighty forest sweeping up to the high line where timber failed and the lofty peaks went up in lonely nakedness against the sky.

"Over there," said Speedy, waving his hand northwest. "That's where we go."

"All right," said Wilson, his voice half stifled, because his teeth were locked by the cold. "And what do we find there?"

"Dupray," said Speedy.

"Dupray?" said Wilson. "What do we want with Charley Dupray?"

"His scalp, that's all," said Speedy calmly.

Wilson was shocked, but he merely grunted.

"Go on, Speedy," he said. "Do a little talking, will you? You want Dupray's scalp. That's all right, but won't you want a regiment of the regular army to get the scalp of Dupray?"

"Maybe," said Speedy. "But that's the fun of it, John."

Wilson cleared his throat, preparatory to speaking, but he did not speak.

Speedy was pleased.

"I'll tell you a yarn, John," he said.

"Go ahead."

"I used to know," continued Speedy, "an old trapper by the name of Eric Langton. He trapped in the mountains, not such a long distance from here. He was a fine old man of about sixty. Straight as a rod; strong as a mountain lion. I used to drop in on him, now and then. One time, when I needed to lay up for a while, I went to visit old Langton, and spent three weeks with him. I would have stayed longer, but at the end of three weeks, when I came back from hunting, one evening, I found that the fire hadn't been lighted in the stove, and supper wasn't ready.

"The cabin was dark. I lighted the lantern, and then I saw Langton lying in a corner, with his head propped up against some stove wood, and both hands clasped over his breast. There was blood all over the floor. His eyes were open, but they were glazed. I thought that he was dead, but there was too much will in him to let him die until I'd come back, and he'd had a chance to tell me his story."

"Go on," said John Wilson, as Speedy paused. "This yarn of yours is as cold as the night air. But go on!"

"Well," said Speedy, "I saw that he was so far gone that I

didn't even dare to give him a drink of whisky to brace him up. I simply squatted by him, and put my ear against his lip. He made a faint whispering sound. But it was simply breath— no articulation in it. Then it occurred to me that perhaps he'd be able to write. I grabbed a piece of paper and put it on a magazine in front of him; then I pushed a pencil into his hand. The blood ran down off his hand onto the paper. But he was able to scratch six shaking letters on the paper before the pencil dropped out of his fingers and his head fell over on his shoulder. He was dead.''

"Poor old chap," said Wilson, shaking his head.

"I picked up the paper," said Speedy, "and saw that the six letters, all wobbling and running downhill, made up the name Dupray, and from that minute I knew that I'd never be able to rest, really, till I'd got back at Dupray.''

"Would Dupray go out and murder an old man like that for nothing?" asked Wilson.

"Not Dupray himself, but one of the hungry dogs that works with him. And that puts the fault back on Dupray again, in a way. However, you can see that it wasn't an easy job.''

"Getting at Dupray? I should say not! A job for a crazy man, Speedy! Dupray always has a dozen first-class gunmen around him, hasn't he?''

"Of course, he has," agreed Speedy very cheerfully. "And I've always known that it was too much for any one man to turn the trick. I had to have help. Not a bunch of men to try to find Dupray's gang—numbers will never locate a fox like that!—but one good man to guard my back, so to speak. You understand? When I saw you stand up before that gang of big lumbermen, I knew that I'd found my man at last. Tell me, John, am I right?''

Wilson did not answer at once. But then, resolutely thrusting out his head, with his jaw set, he muttered: "Speedy, I owe something a lot more than life to you. And I'll never say 'No' to you while there's life in my body!''

# 22

Never did a man hear an answer which was at once so pleasing and so displeasing. It conveyed to Speedy every suggestion of personal devotion; it also showed heroic determination, more almost than Speedy desired to find.

He was, in fact, silent for a moment after Wilson had spoken. Then he said: "I'm thanking you for that, John. I can't ask for more than that."

"Don't thank me for words," said John Wilson abruptly. "Words are cheap and easy enough. Wait till I've actually done something for you, instead of merely talking about it."

"All right," said Speedy, nodding his head.

He pressed his feet into the stirrups and tightened the grip of his knees against the barrel of the mustang. Then he drew in a great breath of the cold, pure air. His respect for John Wilson swelled in his heart; yet his trouble increased, also. He wanted to find a strain of weakness in the man; and that strain would not, it seemed, appear.

As they rode on down the broken, winding trail, John Wilson asked: "You never got up against Dupray before this, Speedy?"

"Never got up against him?" repeated Speedy. "Why, John, I've had a few run-ins with the Dupray people. They operate on a pretty big scale and I've had run-ins with them, well enough."

"Anything bad?"

"Well, I don't know what you'd call bad," murmured Speedy. "The worst was with Lee Purvis, I suppose."

"I don't think I ever heard of Lee Purvis."

"Not many people had, even when Lee was alive," said Speedy. "He was a modest sort of a fellow, but he was wonderful, too."

"Wonderful about what?"

"About precious stones. Diamonds, emeralds, rubies, sapphires, pearls. He knew all about 'em, including how to get them without digging them out of a mine.''

"Jewel thief, you mean?''

"It's hard,'' said Speedy, "to call an artist like Lee Purvis a plain thief. No, he wasn't exactly a thief, though he did a good deal of stealing. I suppose that all of his thefts, added together, would have been worth a couple of million. It was a pretty sad year that didn't see Lee Purvis on the long end of some hundred or two-hundred-thousand-dollar deal.''

He broke off speaking and threw his head back slightly. He seemed to be drinking in the beauty of that night sky, or perhaps he was dreaming about the glorious exploits of Lee Purvis in the past.

Said his companion: "Go on, Speedy. Don't cut me off short like this. How did you get interested in the game?''

"Why,'' said Speedy, "that was when Lee stole the Windover jewels. I knew Tom Windover, and his whole share of the inheritance was in the stones. Above half a million of 'em; the biggest haul that Lee Purvis had ever made. Tom was a pretty sick man, at that time. He had a couple of youngsters. His ranch wasn't paying very well. When the jewels were stolen, it looked pretty hopeless for him. I saw him, about that time, and he told me all about the stones. So I started off on the trail.''

"And got 'em, eh?'' said Wilson.

"The trouble was,'' said Speedy, "that Lee Purvis was hooked up with Dupray in that deal. When I started catching up with Lee, a lot of hurdles were pushed across my path, and Dupray's gang was putting them there.''

"Hurdles like gunmen in the way, eh?'' commented the other.

"Yes, that and other things,'' said Speedy. "But finally I got my hands on the stuff. Then they chased me, pretty closely, too, John. They killed the horse that I was riding, drove me into the rocks, and cornered me on the edge of a ravine with a thousand feet of cliff dropping away behind my back.

"Well, I lay there for three days, without food or water, frying in the sun. But on the third night, a thunderstorm rolled over the mountains and darkened the moon for me. So I started to climb down the rocks. Dupray's fellows, with Lee Purvis among 'em, seemed to guess that I might try that trick, so they lined up along the cliff, after rushing my rock nest and finding the bird gone. They fired at me by the lightning flashes and nicked me a couple of times, but not enough to stop me from climbing; then, as they saw that I was getting away, Lee Purvis got nervous and began to follow me. Of course, the rocks were slippery with the rain water, and Lee had a fall that ended him, poor fellow.

"I found him at the bottom of the cliff when I got down into the ravine below. Poor Lee! There was an artist for you, partner. But, as I was saying, that was the worst run-in that I ever had with Dupray and his men. Dupray was there with them, that night. He's promised a tidy little fortune to any of his men who can snag me and show him the proof that I'm gone. There's only one proof that will really satisfy him, however."

"What's that?"

"My head," said Speedy.

Wilson shuddered. "Look here, Speedy," he said, "you don't mean to say that you'll try to break in on Dupray's gang, when half of them know you by sight, do you?"

"It's not the old Speedy that they'll be seeing, though," said he. "I expect to change my face."

"You're going to trust to a disguise, among those expert crooks?" exclaimed John Wilson.

"Well, why not? With a patch of plaster to make a scar on my face, for instance, and a little dark stain."

Wilson threw up his hands. "A made-up scar, you say? Anybody could see through such a disguise as that."

"I know what you mean," answered Speedy. "The fact is that most patch scars are clumsy affairs. But I've worked for years to make mine correct. Sun and water won't wash it off, John. And I know how the skin gathers along the edge of the cut, and I think that I can deceive even a physician. At least, I have deceived 'em a good many times."

"But Dupray and his men, they're experts, Speedy. You surely wouldn't trust to a disguise."

The growth of horror in his companion began to please Speedy more and more. "Trust me, John," said he cheerfully. "I'll fool the Dupray gang, now that I have you to go along with me. You'll be the boss, and I'll be the servant—your peon. How's that?"

"How am I to pass myself off, so that we can get at the Dupray outfit? And what are we to do when we get there?" asked Wilson.

"I'll tell you," said Speedy. "I know a little village in the mountains, yonder, and in that village there's a small inn. In the inn's yard there's a garden, and that garden runs back to a wall built against the rubble and loose stones of the hillside— built as far back as the conquistadores, in the centuries when they were spilled across this part of the world. There's an old iron door, they say, set into the side of that wall; beyond the wall, in those old days, there used to be a passage of some sort dug into the heart of the mountain. At least, there's a bell still fastened over the arch of the gate, and people in the village say, if any man dares to ring that bell just at sunset, a lot of strange things will be sure to happen to him."

"That sounds like a lot of nonsense to me," said the other calmly.

"It may sound like a lot of nonsense," said Speedy, "but my idea is that that bell and that door are the way to enter the Dupray gang—if they want to take you in!"

"And I'm to ring that bell at sunset?" queried Wilson.

"You'll have the nerve to do it, I know," said the other.

"I'll try it, I suppose," muttered Wilson.

"All that happens," said Speedy, "is that they give you a few tests, I suppose—courage, marksmanship and that sort of thing."

"Humph," said John Wilson. "And if I get through, what about you?"

"Why," said Speedy, "you're a gentleman so used to having service that wherever you go, your servant will have to go, also."

# 23

Red Rock had been an Indian stronghold in the old days; there were still remains of the rude stone walls at the top of the big hill that overlooked the place. Then it had become a Spanish possession, and the Spaniards had built a stone blockhouse on the same hill, but inside the old Indian wall. The ruins of the fort made a picturesque gesture against the sky.

The town of Red Rock, which was both American and Mexican, lay down in the valley itself, and it was composed equally of Mexican dobe houses and American frame ones.

So Red Rock was a combination; and it rambled and scrambled over the floor of the little, narrow valley at its will.

In Red Rock, the arrival of every stranger was an event, at least to the children. And now they came out to stare at the two riders, for it was not every day that they had a chance to look at a master so magnificent or a servant so deformed.

Big John Wilson rode on a splendid chestnut half-bred gelding. His manner, his bearing, his great size, the quality of his horse were enough to fill the eyes of the gamins of Red Rock. But after an admiring glance at him, they turned their attention to Speedy, who rode to the rear.

He was disguised as Jessica Wilson had seen him in San Lorenzo; that is to say, his skin was darkened; his forelock fell down to his eyes, a ragged straw hat was on his head, ragged trousers covered his legs only to the knees and his thin brown shanks descended to worn sandals. He rode humped over a little, like one who has spent most of his life on foot, rather than in the saddle, as was customary in that part of the world.

But his face was the chief attraction. There was a scar, it appeared, that began near the left eye and curved down the side of the face, ending quite close to the back of the jaw. It was a great scar and an old one. One could tell its age by the whiteness of the seam. And it pulled on the skin, which appeared polished and sleek over the cheekbone and exercised a considerable pull upon the eye and the mouth.

A rabble of the youngsters danced and pranced beside Speedy, while they poked their fun at him and twisted their faces into hideous contortions in imitation of the deformity.

He paid no attention.

Presently one of them picked up a stone out of the dust and threw it with a good aim, full at the head of the rearward rider. A slim brown hand flashed up, caught the stone in full flight, and caused it to disappear. And still Speedy appeared to pay no heed.

There was a yell of surprise at this accident or exhibition of skill. Again and again, the stones were thrown at Speedy, but all, in exactly the same manner, were caught out of the air by the same flashing brown hands; and still he kept his head straight forward and looked as stupid as ever.

It was very plain that this was a game and that he enjoyed it, however.

A big lout of fifteen caught up a stone that filled his fist, and it not only had sufficient weight to crack a skull with even a glancing blow, but there was great strength in the arm of the boy. However, an odd thing happened just as he was poising the rock. The hand of Speedy flicked out and a sizable pebble which he had caught a few minutes before was flung with unerring aim.

It cracked against one of the shins of the big youth with such force that he let out a yelp, like a dog when a careless foot steps on its tail.

The rock dropped from his hand. He began to dance about on one foot, holding the hurt place of the injured shin with both hands, and his cruel young companions, like so many wolves, yelled and roared with laughter at his bad luck.

They broke off their yelling, however, and the hurt lad forgot his pain and came limping after the rider of the mustang, gaping, and then shouting with joy. For a miracle was happening.

Out of the agile hands of Speedy a fountain of stones was rising. They danced in the light of the afternoon sun, and they fell into his hands only to rise again. They formed varying shapes and designs. They flowed in an arch. They spouted high and fell to right and left, and presently the speed of the hands was so great that they disappeared from the eye, like the whirring wings of a hummingbird.

Tremendous shouts of applause followed this exhibition, which continued until they drew up in front of the old inn.

There they dismounted, and the stones disappeared in the pocket of Speedy as he hurried forward to hold the head of his master's horse.

There he stood patiently, until a servant came out from the

inn at a dogtrot, to say that the master had found a room and that he would show the way to the stable.

There was a patio, with the stable on one side of it, the inn on the other side, and Speedy soon saw the two horses put up and feed of wretched, sunburned hay pitched into the manger. Then he was led into the hotel and shown the room which Wilson had selected.

For Wilson there was a bed. For the servant, a pair of sheepskins were thrown on the floor. They would serve as both bed and covering. No, there was a straw pallet, brought at Wilson's insistence, and the big sheepskins, skins of the fine mountain sheep, were stretched over it. Supper, it appeared, would be ready just after sunset. Then they were left alone.

Their window looked over the garden at the back of the inn, and from that window big John Wilson stared at the arch of the doorway in the wall. This wall held back the earth and rock that otherwise would have caved in from the hillside to the very door of the inn. The face of the door was dark; it looked the iron that Speedy had declared it to be. Above it, with a rope of cloth hanging down under it, was a large bell.

Wilson continued to stare. The garden was empty, except for one elderly man who sat on a bench in the sun, with something to drink in a glass beside him, while he read his newspaper with his wide-brimmed straw hat tilted back to keep out the slant rays.

Speedy was busily working, laying out the pack of Wilson, when the latter said: "Don't carry on that nonsense of being a servant, Speedy, when we're alone."

"It's better to keep inside the part, whether there's an eye looking at you or not," said Speedy.

"Tell me one thing," said Wilson.

"Yes?"

"Why did you do the juggling? What was that for, Speedy? Won't it call too much attention to you?"

"People, pretty soon," said Speedy, "may start asking why you insist on having me with you, even when you're on the other side of that iron door. Well, they might as well know that I have a pair of hands and know how to do a few things with them. It will save you from a lot of explanations, perhaps. Besides, it amused me."

"It will be sunset in an hour or more," said Wilson, "and that's the time for us to ring the bell, isn't it?"

"Yes, of course."

"Then we'd better put our heads together and do some planning," suggested Wilson.

"There's nothing to plan," said Speedy. "We've talked everything over once, and if we talk it over again, we'll only confuse ourselves. I'm going to have a nap."

Instantly he was stretched out on the pallet of straw, with a sheepskin over him and his eyes closed.

# 24

Wilson, regarding him rather grimly, made sure that his companion was actually asleep. His eyes were not only closed, but ten seconds afterward his chest was rising and falling with a gentle regularity. Wilson looked down on the smaller man with both awe and wonder.

Then he went back to the window and remained there, his elbows resting on the deep casement, staring at the iron door for some minutes.

Nothing had changed in the garden; the man sat on the same bench. Nothing had altered about him, not even in the crossing of his legs, except that the red liquid in the glass had diminished.

Wilson went back to his own bed and sat down on the edge of it. He drew out his revolver, cleaned it carefully, reloaded it, and then looked to the big, long-bladed hunting knife which he carried.

Even with both of those tried weapons, he could not feel secure, and yet Speedy, with empty hands, with nothing but the strength of his slender body, was prepared to face the danger!

Suppose, in spite of the disguise, that they should recognize him. Suppose that someone looked hard at the right profile, disregarding the left, and in spite of the darkness of the skin recognized something of the fine features of this strange youth?

These ideas were crowding through the mind of Wilson when a light hand fell on his shoulder.

He leaped to his feet. He barely kept himself from shouting aloud, and there he found Speedy, standing beside him, with the grotesquely distorted face and grave eyes.

"It is time, señor," said Speedy.

"How did you get off that pallet without making the straw in it crackle?" asked Wilson, breathing hard from the shock he had had.

"Patience and prayer," said Speedy soberly, "accomplish many things. Otherwise, I cannot tell how it was done, señor."

Wilson muttered something to himself, clapped his hat on his head, and gave it a jerk to bring it well down over his eyes.

Through the casement, he saw that the garden wall was red-gold in the sunset light, and the bell above the iron door was gilded likewise.

He was not sixty seconds, perhaps, from the strangest adventure that he had ever met, and the most dangerous. But, squaring his shoulders and drawing in a deep breath, Wilson made a sign of his hand and nodded.

"We'll start, Speedy," said he.

Then he strode first through the door, the perfect picture of a master, down the stairs, and through the short corridor into the garden.

The man with the newspaper lowered it, looked at them, folded the paper and looked again.

A second drink seemed to have been brought to him, for the glass was half full again.

He sipped, detached a cigarette from one of the little bundles of handmade ones which were tied to the brim of his straw hat, and lighted it. Through a cloud of thin smoke, he continued to observe the two strangers. Wilson stopped before him.

"What does that door open on, amigo?" he asked.

The man with the straw hat shook his head.

"Nothing," he said.

"Well," said Wilson, "I've heard that there's really something behind it."

"Perhaps, señor," said the Mexican. "One never knows. The gold that a man hunts for may all the while be in the rocks on which he has built his house. As for me, I know nothing."

"What's the bell for that hangs over it?" asked John Wilson.

"As for me, señor," said the other, "I was raised well and taught to answer all the questions whose answers I know. As for those I do not know, I give you my regrets, señor, and commend you to heaven—with your servant!"

He took off his hat, as he spoke, and revealed a thatch of thick, iron-gray hair on his head.

But John Wilson had an idea, and a very shrewd one, that the bow of the Mexican was chiefly to cover a leering smile, some traces of which still showed in his face as he straightened himself again.

Once more Wilson looked at the door before him, and then strode straight up to it. There was no doorknob to it. He shrugged his shoulders and suddenly laid his hand on the rag of worn, rotting rope extending from the bell.

As he gripped it, a sharp cry from the inn went through him like the edge of a knife.

He jerked his head over his shoulder and saw first the distorted face and the calm eyes of Speedy; and beyond Speedy, there was the dim image of a woman's figure disappearing from the dark arch of the window of the very room which they had just left.

His blood went cold and his brain grew dizzy.

However, his hand was already on the rope, and now he jerked it down.

The bell was cracked, and the result of the strong tug was merely a dull, unmusical, toneless reverberation that sounded like hollow mockery to the ear of John Wilson.

He made a step back from the iron panel.

"This is all nonsense, Speedy," said he.

"Well, perhaps it is," muttered Speedy, "but that name—"

A shudder went through Wilson, as he realized that he had used the forbidden name that would reveal the identity of Speedy in case an ear were pressed close to the inside of that doorway.

"I'll try again," said Wilson gloomily. "But it seems to me just a lot of rot."

He stepped forward, grasped the rope, and then the voice of Speedy stopped him.

"If there is nothing but the hillside to hear, señor, why should we wake up the stone with our noise."

Then, suddenly, soundlessly, as though upon well-oiled hinges, the door opened.

Jet-black darkness was within that doorway, and whoever had opened it was invisible.

"Well?" said John Wilson.

He turned his head, and saw that the man of the straw hat had disappeared, leaving his half-finished glass of wine, if wine it were.

A sudden sense of chilly mystery swept over the soul of John Wilson.

"Well, Pedro," he said, "there's the door open, at last. And nothing to see inside."

"Señor," said Speedy, "you observe that we are no longer inside it, do you not?"

"I observe," Wilson started to say angrily, and then he remembered that, after all, it was not a real servant who stood at his heels, but one whose hints were orders. He settled his hat more firmly on his head and strode through the doorway.

Instantly it clanged heavily behind him!

# 25

Wilson, in the darkness, had out his gun instantly. He stepped back, put his shoulders against the cold of the iron door, and stared into the swimming blackness before his eyes. But there was nothing to be seen, no light whatever, except the red gleams which his own excited imagination called up.

He strode forward a few steps and bumped his head on the low ceiling of the passage. His elbows touched the sides of the tunnel—rough pebbles and dirt that brushed away and fell rattling about his feet.

Then a sudden, powerful sense of stifling came on him. His

heart raced; he choked. If Speedy were only there, to take charge, to tell him what to do! But what could even Speedy suggest at a time like this?

He started forward again, keeping one hand raised above his head to ward off another collision, and worked gradually on until he thought he heard the light crunch of a footfall on the gravel path behind him.

He tried to turn, but his shoulders were wedged in tight. A light flashed, with a little ringing sound of metal, as though the shutter of a bull's-eye lantern had been pushed back, and at the same instant a blow crushed against the back of his head. He pitched forward into more utter darkness.

When he opened his eyes, flames were whirling before them. No, it was only the dull glow of a lantern that fell upon his face.

And then a voice said above him: "He's coming around."

He tried to move his hands, but found that the wrists were bound stiffly together with rope that cut painfully into his skin.

He was lying, he discovered, in a small shack. The air was warmed by a fire in a small cooking stove on top of which a pot steamed. There was the fragrance of coffee through the place. Instantly it made him hungry, so hungry that he forgot the pain in his head.

He lay on a damp, earthen floor. Seated on a stool beside him, was a man in a blue flannel shirt with a cartridge belt strapped around his hips and a Colt in a leather holster weighing it down at one side. He was a broad chunk of a man, nursing a short-stemmed pipe in a hand that had a blue anchor printed across the back of it, the anchor chain disappearing up the sleeve of the shirt.

"He's comin' around, Bones," said the watcher.

"Let him come, Sid," said the other.

John Wilson turned his head.

On the other side of the shack was the second speaker, "Bones," tall and gaunt enough to warrant the use of that nickname. There was always a smile on his face, owing to the outthrust of a large pair of upper teeth, but the wrinkles around the eyes and the gleam of the eyes themselves gave no hint of good nature. He worked with rapid, deft fingers at the construction of a horsehair braid that might become, later on, part of a bridle, perhaps.

His shirt was blue flannel, like Sid's, but he had added to it the surprising decoration of a red necktie.

"You can sit up, brother," said Sid to Wilson.

The prisoner raised himself, hitched about, and put his back against the wall.

"This is better," he announced calmly.

"Want anything?" asked Sid.

"No," said Wilson, still perfectly calm. "A new head, maybe. That's all."

"That's the trouble with Bones," commented Sid. "Always thinks that the other gent has a head made of iron, like his own."

"Aw, shut your face," said Bones, yawning. "What made you ring the bell, brother?"

"Curiosity," said Wilson.

"And what else?"

"Nothing to tell you."

"I got half a mind to sock you again," said Bones, pausing in his work for the first time, and looking steadily at the captive.

Wilson answered nothing.

"Whacha expect to see, when the door opened and you went into the tunnel?" asked Sid, as Bones industriously resumed the braiding of the horsehair.

"Well," said Wilson, "I expected to see Dupray."

Sid rose, went to the stove, poured out some coffee into a cup, and sipped it.

"Cool, ain't he?" he asked of Bones.

"Yeah, he's cool," said Bones, without looking up.

"He's all-fired cool," said Sid, insisting on the point. "What's your name, brother?"

"That's for Dupray," said Wilson.

"Listen to him," said Sid. "Listen at him, will you? All right, son. You're gonna talk to Dupray. Maybe you'll wish that you hadn't talked, before you're through, though. Here comes the chief now, I guess."

A footfall came up to the door of the cabin and a little man with a pale, round face entered. He looked like a cross

between a man and a frog. To increase the strangeness of his
face, he was wearing a skullcap of black silk which appeared
when he took off his hat. He paused as he entered, and looked
at the prisoner.

"That's the one, eh?" he remarked.

Neither Bones nor Sid answered this question. The new-
comer sat down on the edge of the center table and folded his
hands in his lap. As he looked down at the prisoner, he said:
"You never saw me before, did you?"

"No," said Wilson.

"Who are you, then?"

"I'll tell you when I find out who you are," said Wilson.

Sid observed again: "He's cool, Charley. Look at how cool
he is, and with his head all busted by Bones, a minute ago."

"Shut up," commanded the other.

He added, to Wilson: "Who do you think I am?"

"I think you're Charley Dupray."

"I'm Dupray," said the little man. "Who are you?"

"I'm John Wilson."

"Wilson, or was it Smith that you said, or Jones, or
Brown?" asked Dupray.

His eyes were slits, the pupils shifting almost out of sight
when they moved up and down. He was the ugliest piece of
flesh that ever had been called a man, it seemed to Wilson.

"My name is Wilson," said the captive.

" 'Wilson, that's all,' " said Sid with a grin.

Dupray turned his round, froglike head toward his man,
and Sid stepped a little to the side, as though to get away
from the impact of that glance.

"Your name is Wilson, then," concluded Dupray, as he
looked back at the man on the floor.

"Yes," said John Wilson.

"What brought you up here?"

"I was looking for something to do."

"What?"

"Quick money," said Wilson.

"Going to get your quick money out of me?"

"Yes," said Wilson.

"What makes you think that I'll use you?" said Dupray.

"You can't afford to turn me down," said Wilson. "I'm the stuff that you want."

"What do I want?"

"You want steady nerves; I've got 'em. You want a good rider; I'm that. You want a good shot; I'll stand up to the best."

"You've got a lingo, anyway," declared Dupray. "Where did you hear about me?"

"All over the range."

"Where did you hear about the iron door and the bell?"

"From Speedy," said Wilson.

The foolish words had dropped from his lips involuntarily. His hair lifted on his scalp. His eyes, however, he controlled, keeping them calm and fixed steadily on the face of the other.

The name, Speedy, however, had caused an instant sensation. Bones leaped to his feet; Sid, with an exclamation, actually snatched out a revolver. Even the frog-face of Dupray wrinkled all over with hate as he heard the word.

"Speedy's a friend of yours, is he?" asked Dupray.

"He used to be," said Wilson.

"What made him a friend?"

"He pulled me out of a hole once."

"How was that?"

"I was having some trouble with a fellow called Slade Bennett."

"You knew Slade Bennett?" asked Dupray, his eyes gleaming again.

"Yes. Pretty well, but not for long."

"How did you come to know him?"

"By fighting him."

"He dropped you, eh?"

"No, I killed him," said the prisoner.

"He killed Slade Bennett!" breathed Bones.

Only gradually the tall, skinny fellow reseated himself, his eyes round as they stared at the captive.

"You say you killed Bennett. I remember, now, it was a man named Wilson that killed Slade. Slade was my friend."

Dupray paused for an answer.

But Wilson merely shrugged his shoulders, as though words were not necessary. He added: "Well, Bennett picked the fight. But that doesn't matter. I'm glad I bumped him off."

For the first time, Dupray smiled a little. And the expression did not make his face more attractive.

"You killed my friend, Bennett; Speedy sent you up here; and still you think you can have a place with me?" he asked.

"If I didn't think that," said Wilson, "why would I have come?"

Even the inhuman, cold eyes of Dupray were opened a little by the blunt shock of this question.

"Because you're a fool, perhaps," said he.

"Because," said Wilson, "I didn't think you were fool enough to have a man like me tapped on the head by way of introduction to your crowd. But I'm going to come in, Dupray, and I'm going to bring my servant in with me!"

# 26

Dupray, with the tip of a pale-red tongue, moistened his lips, and all the time he looked at Wilson with eyes as thoughtful as those of a cat when it considers a helpless mouse.

"Bluff won't work up here," he said, shaking his head at last.

"Do you call this a bluff?" asked Wilson.

And he lifted his bound hands.

"Speedy," said Dupray. "How long have you known him?"

"I knew him for three days," said Wilson. "Afterward, he got tired of me."

"What made him tired?"

"He didn't like the way I treated my wife."

"How did you treat her?"

"I left her."

"Why?"

"I couldn't stand the ranch life. Riding herd, and that sort of business, it was nothing for me."

"And what makes you think that you can come in here with

a body servant?'' asked Dupray, tilting his head a little to one side.

"Because you'll want me; and because I'm used to having somebody to look after me.''

"He's got a nerve, is what he's got,'' said Bones. "A servant, eh?''

"What can this peon do—what's his name?''

"Pedro.''

"What can he do, then?''

"Cook, make a patch, sew on buttons, clean knives and guns, cut up game, roll cigarettes.''

"You can't roll your own, eh?'' said Dupray, sneering.

"Pedro can roll 'em better,'' said Wilson.

"I'm going to take in Pedro so that you won't have to roll your own? What else can the fool do?''

It was plain that Dupray was much irritated. "He can do anything that he's needed for,'' said Wilson. "Including putting a knife in anybody's throat.''

"Oh, he's a knife expert, is he?''

"He is. He can stand five paces off and hit a mark half an inch wide with a knife.''

"He can't,'' said Dupray.

"He can, though,'' argued Wilson.

He cast back in his mind. At five paces, a line half an inch long dwindles so that it looks hardly more than a pencil stroke. Was it possible that Speedy could actually hurl a knife and strike it? He felt that he had overshot the mark a good deal in making this boast.

"Suppose that I believe you,'' said Dupray, "and you bring in the peon, Pedro, and let him try his hand at hitting a half-inch mark at five paces!''

He grinned with sudden malice, as he made the suggestion.

"Well?'' said Wilson.

"If he can do that two times out of three, even,'' said Dupray, "then I'll believe the other lies that you've been telling me, and I'll take you into the band, let you have this Pedro to take care of you like a baby in the cradle, if you wish. But if—''

He paused, and was lost a moment in thought.

"But,'' he repeated, "if he fails, I'll cut his throat before your eyes and cut yours afterward. That's all. Bones, go get the peon!''

He turned his back on the prisoner at this and, sitting down close beside the stove, he held out his gray hands to the warmth of it, though already the room was quite hot. More than ever, he seemed to big John Wilson a mere cold-blooded creature and not human at all.

This was the Dupray of whom, along the latter part of the journey, Speedy had told such strange tales! This was the man who had made fortune after fortune and piled up treasure which, it was said, he never spent—a bloodless miser, who increased his store and gloried only in money for the sake of money.

Well, this was a strange world, it seemed to John Wilson. There was Speedy, who looked like a too-handsome stripling, good for nothing but charming to the ladies, with the soul of a demon and the cunning of a cougar.

The minutes passed.

Not a person in the cabin moved except Sid, who occasionally, as he stood at the open door, turned and glanced at the captive, then gave his attention once more to the outdoors.

Finally he said: ''All right. They're here.''

''Both?'' said Dupray.

''Both,'' said Sid.

He stepped back from the door, and through it came Speedy; as he stood blinking a little at the lantern light, he saw Wilson.

''El señor!'' he cried and, throwing out his hands, he leaped for Wilson.

Sid, without a word, struck that leaping figure solidly on the side of the head and knocked Speedy flat on the floor.

Dupray had regarded the whole scene over his shoulder, unconcerned.

''That's all right, Sid,'' said he. ''Pick the fool up. Draw a half-inch line on the door, Bones. Half an inch wide and a foot long.''

It was done. Speedy was picked up from the floor and, as he stood with his hands to his head, Wilson said: ''There's no trouble, Pedro. It's only a little test that's to be given you, and I know you can do it. Stand across the cabin floor—and throw a knife into a half-inch mark.''

"Ah," said Speedy, shaking his head, "that is not a wide mark, señor.''

Dupray had turned his back on the scene once more. His hands continued to hover over the hot surface of the stove.

He said: "Pedro, you'll hit that mark, or else I'll have your throat cut first, and your master's throat cut second. Do you understand me?''

"The good saints!" gasped Speedy.

"You'll find Satan more used to this sort of a place," remarked Dupray. "Are you ready?''

Still he did not turn his head, but faced the stove.

"Señor?" said Speedy, holding out pathetic hands to Wilson.

"Pedro," said Wilson, "it is true. You hit the mark two times out of three, or else—''

He paused. The pause said more than words. And the heart of John Wilson fell like a stone. Bones was marking off the five paces, while Speedy cried out, wringing his slender brown-stained hands: "Ah, but you step too far. The paces are altogether too long.''

"He said five paces. He didn't say how long them paces was to be," grinned Bones.

Speedy held up both hands to the ceiling as though to call the saints to witness this injustice. As a matter of fact, it was not fifteen feet, but nearer to twenty where he took his post, near the farther wall of the cabin. Three hunting knives were stuck into a log beside him, ready to his hand.

One moment Speedy murmured, as though repeating a prayer, his eyes closed, his fragile body wavering a little from side to side.

Then, with a quick catch of his breath, he caught up one of the knives and balanced it carefully in the palm of his hand.

There was a partial mist before the eyes of Wilson. It might be that in practice, with nothing depending upon it, Speedy could perform the difficult feat, but surely no human being in the world could do the thing with the chilly eyes of death itself fixed upon him.

But now he was standing with his toe on the mark, and his eyes fixed burningly on the target.

"Put the lantern nearer to the line," he commanded briefly, huskily.

The order was obeyed in silence.

Then, swiftly, the brown hand went back, and the knife slithered out of the palm, struck the door with a distinct shock, and was fixed there, humming like a bee.

Bones leaped to the spot with one bound.

"A miss!" he shouted. "He missed it by a full inch!"


# 27


Speedy had groaned aloud and again threw up his brown hands to implore luck.

It was interesting to note the behavior of the others.

Sid took on an air of real concern and looked with an anxious frown toward the target which Pedro had failed to hit; but Bones was openly exulting as he looked toward the frozen face of John Wilson.

Strangest of all was the behavior of the great Dupray, for he had not turned his head for a single instant, but continued to extend his hands over the stove.

He merely said: "He has two more chances to make his hits. Then we'll do something about it, if he misses!"

Vaguely, John Wilson wondered what would happen. When Pedro missed, the others could not realize that they would have on their hands not a frightened peon, but Speedy himself, raging among them at close quarters. Perhaps he would try to knock over the lantern, first of all, and then to liberate the prisoner and put a weapon in his hand.

But what good would that be, when the force of the ropes had numbed the arms of Wilson almost to the elbow?

At any rate, there was Speedy, balancing the second knife in his hand and giving a little cry as he hurled it, far harder than the first!

Bones did not advance so eagerly this time. He merely leaned a little forward, and growled: "Well, he had some luck, that time. He split the middle of the line!"

"He's getting the range, perhaps," said Dupray.

Still the man did not turn his head, but now he began to rub his cold hands together and feverishly hold them out toward the warmth once more. His whole concern was apparently more to warm his hands than any interest in the death of two men, which was about to be decided by the next cast of a knife!

Swiftly, Speedy picked the third knife from the wall and nursed it for a moment in his cunning right hand, narrowing his eyes toward the mark. Again the hand quickly jerked back, and John Wilson closed his eyes.

He heard the thud of the knife; he heard the hum of it as it quivered in the wood, and then, as that humming died out, there was silence.

That silence seemed to endure for centuries. John Wilson strove to open his eyes, but he could not.

Then said the voice of Bones, in a gasp: "Doggone, he's cut the mark again. There it is, right on the edge of the mark, but in it, all right!"

John Wilson opened his eyes and took a breath. He had been almost stifled during the preceding moments.

Then he saw that Speedy was picking the three knives out of the door and laying them carefully upon the center table.

At this, Dupray turned suddenly from before the stove, strode quickly around the table and, coming up to Speedy, laid the muzzle of a revolver against his breast. His left hand fell upon the shoulder of Pedro, and his eyes were fastened upon him.

"Who are you?" asked Dupray, in English.

"Pedro, señor," said Speedy.

"You lie," said Dupray. "You're acting a part. You're no more afraid than I am. You're not shaking. You're steady as a rock!"

Wilson, staring with horror, saw the truth so rapidly revealed.

Said Speedy: "Why should I be afraid, señor, since two of the three knives hit the mark?"

"Bah!" said Dupray, and thrust him away.

Speedy staggered, seemed to lose balance, and fell back heavily, his shoulders against the wall.

Dupray followed him a single step. His head thrust out.

There was a suggestion of malicious cruelty in his whole attitude.

But suddenly he snapped his fingers and went hastily back to the stove, over which he extended his hands once more.

"I have to take chances on everything," he said, no longer regarding Speedy, now cowering against the door, under the leveled gun of Bones. "I take a chance on you, Wilson. You have nerve enough, and if you're able to do as much, as a man, as Pedro's able to do as a servant, you'll be worth my while. Bones, set him free. Fix him up with a bunk, blankets, anything he wants. I'll see him again in the morning. We ride tomorrow, you know, and we may try the pair of them together on the trip."

He left the stove and went to the door as he spoke. Stepping out into the night without any other farewell, he said, without turning his head: "You can tell them where we ride."

He was gone, even the last words dying out as he continued straight ahead into the darkness.

Bones, for a moment, stared toward the opened doorway; then, with a grunt and a shrug of his shoulders, he approached Wilson and cut the rope that held his hands.

Wilson stood up.

"How are you feeling, partner?" asked Sid.

"Hungry," said Wilson, though that was not the readiest word to his lips.

"Bones, you're the cook," said Sid.

"No, no," said Wilson. "There's Pedro here. A good cook. Pedro," he added in Mexican, "food for the three of us, and enough scraps left over for you, too, at the end!"

Speedy made a gesture of assent and hurried to explore the larder. He found the usual supplies: bacon, white flour, corn-meal, a few potatoes, old, withered onions, some cans of tomatoes, one of plum jam. There was coffee, of course, in plenty.

Straightway he began to busy himself with the food and, as he worked, the strains of an old Mexican song filled his throat and floated softly through the room.

"Shut up that noise!" cried Bones angrily.

John Wilson raised one finger.

"He sings to please me," said he.

"And who in the mischief are you but a doggone recruit?" exclaimed Bones, his smile hardening about his buck teeth.

"Why," said John Wilson, "from this time on, I'm as good as anybody you know, except Dupray. And what about you, Bones? What are you good for?"

Speedy, turning an instant from his cookery, observed the pair of them: Wilson obviously resenting that blow in the dark that had struck him down, and ready enough to fight on account of it, and Bones equally determined not to give ground.

It both raised and depressed the heart of Speedy. If anything were to quell the spirit of John Wilson, what he had just been through seemed enough to have lowered his courage, at least. Instead of that, he seemed as aggressive as ever.

"Gentlemen," said Speedy, cheerfully, "are we not friends, now that we are all together?"

Wilson and Bones continued to glare at one another, but Sid pressed in between them.

"Steady," said Sid. "You boys don't want to make trouble. You've had trouble enough for one night, Wilson. And you, Bones, know what the chief does when anybody starts a fight in camp. Back up, the pair of you!"

"I'll back up when there's somebody able to make me back up," declared Bones. "I'll have more air, in the meantime, while I wait for another day!"

So saying, he stalked out through the door.

# 28

Never were the cunning fingers of Speedy more expert and rapid than in the preparation of that meal! Sid and the new recruit, John Wilson, talked together while Speedy cut the rashers of bacon, making them translucently thin; then he was mixing cornmeal with flour for frying and, after the bacon had become crisp, a shower of transparent slices of potatoes fell into the same pan. In no time at all, the meal was served.

They ate and Sid talked over the meal. It was his second

supper that night, but his appetite was good. It was, he said, something worth while to eat food prepared like this, and for his part he could understand why Wilson carried a servant about with him on his travels. He, Sid, would try the same thing, one day, but where was one to find another Mexican like Pedro?

"They're born like Pedro, not made that way," commented Wilson dryly.

He wanted to know, next, where they were to ride the next day, and Sid told them briefly. It was a simple job. The stage to Red Rock from Cumberland was bringing over a heavy shipment of gold bullion. The point for the holdup had been picked out. The driver of the stage was a greenhand. The guard was a known fool and probably a coward. Sid missed his guess if a single shot would have to be fired, beyond a salvo to bring the stage to a halt. They would soon gut the coach, and take whatever was worthwhile from the passengers.

"But," said Sid, "that ain't what bothers me. It's a dead-easy job, but we oughta leave things alone, as close to home as the Red Rock stage. Everybody'll know that we had a hand in the work. But the way with Charley Dupray is that he can't go and leave his hand off of bullion. Solid gold and solid silver, that's what makes his mouth water. Them things, and jewels.

"And that's why he wants to go after the Red Rock stage. There's been more money aboard it lots of times, but not in gold bullion. It's the real metal that he goes drunk on."

"So that's what we're in on tomorrow?" said John Wilson.

"That's what you're in on," answered the other, nodding.

"Pedro, gimme another slab of them fried potatoes, will you?" Wilson translated swiftly into Spanish and the potatoes were duly brought.

"You teach that peon English," said Sid, "and he'd be worth his weight in gold."

"Rather have him as he is," said Wilson. "You can talk more freely in front of a man that doesn't know your language."

"True," said Sid. "I never somehow thought of that, between you and me."

"It's worth thinking about," commented Wilson. "Is that the moon rising?"

"That's her, all right."

"She looks like a forest fire," said Wilson. "I'll have a look at her."

"Go ahead," answered Sid. "I'll hold down the fried potatoes while you're away."

Wilson got up and stepped through the door and a little distance into the dark, so that he could see to full advantage the rising of the moon in the throat of the pass, soaring slowly up among the great pine trees. By that increasing light he could also see in outline, at least, the wreckage of an old mining camp, the cabins sitting in a huge, irregular circle. In one or two of these, feeble lights glimmered and these, no doubt, were the quarters of the band of Dupray.

Strongly as the mountains fenced in the hollow in which the old camp lay, even more strongly, Wilson felt, he and Speedy were enclosed in the hand of the bandit leader. What gain could come to them, he could not dream.

He was still standing in the brush, watching the rising of the moon when a man came stepping past him to the door of the cabin he had just left.

"Is the chief in there?" asked the stranger, as he came to the open door.

"He's over in the main shack, I guess," answered the voice of Sid, dimly, from the interior.

At once the other turned and tramped away, the brush crackling like burning firewood about his feet. It was not long before a light touch plucked at the sleeve of Wilson.

He turned with a great start, and the voice of Speedy murmured: "Did you see him?"

"The stranger? Yes."

"Not a stranger," said Speedy. "It was the old man from the garden, the fellow with the glass of wine. And he means us, by this trip, I think."

"How could he mean us?" muttered Wilson.

"What else would bring him here in such a hurry, with his eyes sticking out of his head?" said Speedy. "Remember, we left horses and luggage back there at the hotel. They have light fingers and sharp eyes. They may have been able to put two and two together. Hurry! We'll follow him and see what he does."

The form of the stranger was already a mere dark blur in the distance, heading toward one of the lighted cabins, as they began the pursuit.

"Step in my tracks!" Speedy muttered over his shoulder.

Wilson, obeying, found to his bewilderment that he was making no noise whatever, but weaving silently back and forth through the brush.

"What about Sid, left alone in there?" asked Wilson. "He'll grow suspicious."

"There are plenty of fried potatoes to keep Sid from thinking of anything else for quite a time to come," said Speedy. "Don't worry about him. Our worries all lie ahead of us, just now! Unless I'm very far wrong, we'll have our hands full, before you've counted a hundred twice."

They saw the shadow of the stranger pause in front of the dimly lighted doorway of one of the cabins; then the man entered. Speedy increased his pace, and in a moment they were standing at a window.

It had been boarded over to keep out winter wind, but there were plenty of cracks through which they were able to look into the interior.

They saw three men playing cards at a table. One of them was no other than their new acquaintance, Bones. To the side of the table, just rising from a bunk and throwing back his blankets, was the great Dupray, and in front of him stood the stranger—the old man of the garden behind the inn.

Dupray was saying: "I told you never to come up here till you were sent for, or until you had news, real news. What do you mean by it?"

"Señor," said the other, "I have news, indeed!"

A horse whinnied loudly, at this moment, from the shed behind the cabin.

When the noise died down, the messenger was saying: "This is the truth that we found, señor. The small boys in the street saw the man with the scarred face juggle eight stones at once like a performer in a circus. When we examined the luggage that the two left behind them in the hotel, we found in the little bundle that belonged to the man of the scarred face, some new strings for a guitar. Do you understand, señor?''

"A juggler who plays a guitar? Well, what of that?" asked Dupray.

"Is there not a saying," said the old man, bowing a little, "that the north wind can give the sky a hundred faces and that Speedy can assume even more?"

"Speedy!" exclaimed Dupray, going back a step. "A thousand demons! I've grown old and blind. Speedy is in the camp!"

He turned on the three who were rising with stupefied faces from the table.

"Get out and at him!" exclaimed Dupray. "Gather around the cabin. But go like wildcats stalking a mountain lion! Quick! Quick! Don't make a move until I've joined you. Walk on eggs and hold your breath. Don't even whisper! Speedy! Oh, if I can only put a knife in his heart tonight, I'll die happy tomorrow."

As he spoke, that impassive face contorted to a dreadful mask.

The other three hastily left the place, and slowly crossed the brush tangles toward the light that, in the distance, marked the cabin where Speedy and his companion were supposed to be.

Two things filled the mind of Wilson, along with wonder that Speedy did not instantly give the signal for them to flee.

The first was the sight of Dupray removing a little chamois sack from a vest pocket and attaching it to a buckskin thong that was looped around his neck.

The second was that at his ear there was a faint sound of music that made him think that he was turning mad. Then he realized that in fact Speedy was humming, under his breath, the last Mexican tune that Wilson had heard him sing.

"To the door!" murmured Speedy. "Softly, softly!"

As he spoke, he led the way, and they passed rapidly, noiselessly around the corner of the building. At the door Speedy crouched. Running steps came toward them from the interior of the shack. A shadow swept across the threshold; the body of Dupray followed; and then Speedy leaped, as a cat springs, out of the darkness of the ground, and struck Dupray helpless with a blow!

# 29

There was not a groan, not a sound. There was only the dim flurry of Speedy's hands as, with flying fingers, he wound cord around the hands of his captive and inserted the gag between his teeth.

Then he stood up and drew Dupray, also, to his feet.

"Carry him, John," he said to Wilson. "He's heavier than you think, but not too heavy for those shoulders of yours. Steady, now, and in two minutes we're away."

"This way," urged Wilson. "Don't go back toward the danger of—"

"This way," answered Speedy with a dangerous purr in his excited voice. "Are you stopping to argue with me—now?"

Wilson followed, humbled and overawed, while Speedy led the way rapidly around the side of the house, and to the shed behind it, from which neighing had been heard.

"The moon, the cursed light of the moon!" muttered Speedy, fumbling at the latch of the shed. "That makes everything twice as difficult."

The door opened under his hands, and he entered, with Wilson following in haste to get out of the increasing flood of the silver light.

In the hollow cup of his hands, Speedy shielded the match which he had lighted, but allowed sufficient radiance to escape to show the line of sleek-backed horses which stood in a long row before them—a full score of priceless mounts.

Two, at the nearer end, were saddled, one of the pair lying, the other still munching in his manger.

"Good!" murmured Speedy. "Now we have it, John. You never thought, Dupray, that somebody outside your gang would ever thank you for keeping horses saddled and ready?"

Feverish impatience ate up the heart of Wilson.

"Do we take those horses, Speedy?" he asked. "Or do we ride with this Dupray, too? What are we to do with him?"

"We're to take him back to law and order, John," said Speedy, already throwing a saddle on the back of the next horse in line. "Hold him fast. We—"

He had slid the bridle over the head of the tall horse and was drawing up the cinches, when the ears of John Wilson were split by a bloodcurdling shriek from the throat of his captive:

"Help! This way! Help! The stables!"

The first yell so startled him that it was not until he had allowed those six words to escape that he clapped his hand over the mouth of the other.

His hand was promptly bitten to the bone!

He snatched it back and struck the face of Dupray brutally. He was rewarded by feeling the body go limp in his arms.

He kicked open the door behind him and flung the limp weight over the saddle on the back of one horse, while he himself sprang into a second saddle.

Before them, an uproar of shouting had broken out.

As Wilson mounted, he was aware of shadows running toward them through the moonlight. A volley of bullets hummed through the air above them, about them. And there was the voice of Speedy, calling: "Spur, John, spur!"

So they rushed down the hollow, neck to neck, Wilson on one side of the limp body of the outlaw, and Speedy on the other.

At the throat of the ravine, the tumult was dying out behind them. The firing had ceased, for a thick screen of trees and brush quite shut them from the sight of the gang.

Then they halted long enough to right their captive in his saddle. As he recovered consciousness, he made an effort, sat up straight, and cursed them with a low breath.

But Speedy was already tying the feet of Dupray into the stirrups. It was the best way to make sure of his careful riding. He might try to throw himself to the ground in the midst of the pursuit, otherwise. That maneuver he would never attempt, however, if it meant being dragged along the ground under the trampling hoofs of the horse.

When they had their captive secure, gagged once more, lest he should guide the pursuit by a yell at the critical moment, they rode on again, but not at full speed. There

were two things against that, Speedy said. In the first place
they did not know the trail perfectly. In the second place,
nothing saps the strength and wind of a horse so much as to
run it suddenly at full speed before it has a chance to grow
warm with work, particularly in the cold of mountain air.

And what cold it was!

As they climbed the next hill, they could see a dozen dark
forms of riders streaming over the ridge of the hill behind, in
sharp pursuit.

But still Speedy would not allow them to ride at full speed.

"They're catching up with us, Speedy!" shouted Wilson.
"Do you see?"

The last frantic question was like a bullet kicking up the
dust of the road before them.

"Pull down to a trot for this grade," was the calm
command of Speedy in answer.

And Wilson, overcome by a wave of horror and awe,
obeyed in spite of himself.

All the rest had been nothing, compared with the time they
spent trotting their horses up that grade, while a host of
yelling demons flogged and spurred their frantic horses after
them, and Dupray rode with his head turned, fiercely devouring
that hope.

No, nothing else was of the slightest account.

Was he, Wilson, a man who loved danger? Never, if
danger meant zest gained by an experience such as this! An
utter sickness came over him, and then a blind, rioting panic.
He hardly knew what he was doing as he put the spurs into
the tender flanks of his horse. Not until the dark crest of the
hill rose like the crest of a wave between him and the pursuit,
not until that moment did he realize that he had abandoned a
tried comrade in the hour of need.

But what need was there for loitering at the jaws of death,
as Speedy had chosen perversely to do?

He pulled back to a hand gallop, and then saw Speedy and
the form of Dupray beside him, swing over the crest, still at a
trot, and then break into a swift gallop down the incline.

Behind them, hardly a moment away, came the others,
charging. And every rider of them was firing as he came!

Well, they were shooting from very irregular firing platforms, for one thing, and at swiftly moving targets for another. Now, suddenly, they began to fall behind. They left off shooting. They were devoting all their efforts to flogging and spurring their spent horses to a greater effort.

Speedy drew alongside, and still he was keeping his horse well in hand. The moon struck on the face of Dupray and showed the silent agony that contorted it, as he gave up the last hope.

Out of the shame and the bitterness of his heart, Wilson cried out: "Speedy, forgive me if you can!"

"Forgive you?" called Speedy cheerfully. "Why, man, everybody loses his head once in a lifetime, at least. Besides, I may have drawn it a bit fine. I thought their hands would be too cold for straight shooting off a galloping horse, though!"

# 30

They were through the pass and had got down in the valley, with the wide lowlands spread before them and San Lorenzo marked in white on the horizon, their road winding pleasantly over an easy, level plain. Wilson rode at the side of the frog-faced man; Speedy was in the rear, as always. But now he rode up and said to his friend: "Look here, John. I didn't show you these."

He picked from his pocket a small chamois sack.

"This is what Dupray tied under his shirt. I took it away from him while we were scuffling around. And it's no wonder that he preferred to wear the stuff nearest to his heart!"

As he spoke, he turned the little sack upside down, and out of the open mouth of it streamed a shower of blood-red rubies onto his palm.

"Just in case Charley Dupray should find himself shipwrecked on a desert island," murmured Speedy. "This would fill his eye and his dull moments; it would fill the eye of any jeweler in the world, too. Look at this big fat one with the bright face. How would that do as a pendant, or to put into the business end of a king's scepter, eh?"

"It's a beauty," said John Wilson, nodding his head,

"Not very many in the world better than this, are there, Charley?" asked Speedy.

The criminal turned his head, looked at the great stone for a moment, and then jerked his eyes away again, as though he could not endure to see the stone in another hand.

"I'll tell you this, Speedy," said Dupray, "I can take you to a place where you'll find enough jewels to make that heap in your hand look like nothing at all. You could have the lot of 'em—all the jewels and all of the hard cash."

He passed the pale, pink tip of his tongue over his blood-less lips. It was like the rapid flicker of the tongue of a snake. He shuddered, in spite of the heat of the sun.

"I tell you what, Speedy, I'll pay you everything in the treasure, if you'll let me have my life and that one ruby."

"Do you mean that?" asked Speedy.

"It's not that the stone is worth so very much money," said Dupray. "That isn't it, man. It's only that I'm used to that ruby. You understand? My eye's used to it; my eye loves it. You're a sensitive man, Speedy, or I couldn't talk to you like this. But you'll understand me when I speak to you like this, straight out of the heart. I drench the pair of you with wealth and, in exchange, you give me nothing but my freedom and that one stone!"

"Charley," said Speedy, "why didn't you make us an offer long ago, before we got down into the plain?"

"Because," said Dupray, "I knew that you never intended to take me to the jail, really. Of course, I knew that nobody would turn me in when he had a chance to get my money. I was waiting for you to name your price. That was all. But, now that we've got as close to San Lorenzo as this, I see that you are going to hold me up for the whole lot!"

"Suppose that we put you in prison, in spite of your treasures," said Speedy. "Suppose we jail you, and let your treasure rot, eh?"

The frog-face grew white, and the eyes shut for an instant. Then they opened and Dupray said: "You've got half a million, say, in that handful. You fools, how many other handfuls do you think I have? I can dip in and choose where I wish. Rubies? Yes. What about yellow topaz, though? Yellow as golden fire. Then there's a great flat-headed sapphire that would make you think of a lake in the mountains and—"

He stopped suddenly, for he found that the eye of Speedy was resting upon him with infinite pity and mercy and understanding as well; yet there was inexorable justice waiting in that eye, also.

"You mean to run me in, then, and let the stuff go to waste?" asked Dupray.

"If you had all the money in the world, if that mountain were one diamond, and you owned it all," said Speedy, "I wouldn't turn you loose. Because I know you, Dupray, and you're not a man, but an evil spirit. You look like a ghoul, and you are one. You're the only man I ever knew that I could hate with my whole heart. There's no kindness, gentleness, good faith, or anything human about you. You're going to prison, and you'll walk out of that place to hang—unless the mob tears down the walls to get at you first."

He said this so calmly that big John Wilson could hardly give credence to his ears. But he realized, then, that Speedy was inexorable in his determination. He realized, too, that money was no real temptation to this strange man.

But no smile came on the face of Speedy until they had seen the steel door of a cell close on Dupray, leaving that hideous frog-face in the shadow. Not once had Dupray spoken since Speedy had given him his answer. But hatred spoke in his silence more clearly than in his talk.

They went from the jail to the hotel.

"I'm ashamed to face Jessica," said John Wilson. "When I look back, I feel that I've been a dog. I don't dare to face her, Speedy!"

"Why should you feel that way?" said Speedy. "You told her that you wanted to go out and make a fortune for yourself, and you've done that. I've an idea that none of those rubies—except maybe the big fellow, there—can be identified, and so they'll belong to you and me, old son. And your half ought to be eighty or a hundred thousand. That's something of a fortune, isn't it? That'll enable you to hold your head up and look your father-in-law in the face, no matter how rich he may be."

"It's true," said Wilson. "But there's more than money to give her."

"What?" asked Speedy, curiously.

"A new idea," said Wilson. "I can give her that. Because I was rather a restless fellow, when you found me, Speedy, but I left all that restlessness back there in the moonlight on the slope of that hill, where you kept the horses at a trot, with all those demons galloping up behind us."

He shivered, then shrugged his shoulders to get rid of the memory.

"Go out into the garden. She'll be down by the river at this time of day," said Speedy, as they turned into the entrance of the hotel.

He himself followed on more slowly. He was still within the shadow of the garden gate when he heard a girl's voice cry out joyously. And in that joyous cry Speedy himself could find a measure of reward and of thankfulness.

# Part Three

# 31

Cort swept in his winnings and collected the cards to deal again, when his companion shook his head, pushed back his chair, and stood up with a jingle of spurs.

"I'm busted," said he.

The concern which William Cort showed was entirely professional in its smoothness but, like many experienced gamblers in the West, though he had not the slightest scruple in palming cards or running up a pack, he made it a practice to return some of the feathers whenever he had stripped a victim bare.

"Flat broke?" asked Cort. "Well then, take a twenty for luck," said Cort, pushing the money across the table.

His victim picked up the money, hesitated, and then put it down again.

"My luck's out at cards," he explained, "and twenty dollars' worth of whisky won't be good for my liver. Keep the coin, brother. I don't mind losing it, but the game was kind of short. That's the only trouble."

Cort picked up the money again with a graceful gesture of regret and glanced over the faces of those who were lingering in the corner of the saloon to watch the game.

"Anybody take a hand?" he asked. "Plenty of you to make up a game of poker," he added.

But Cort's manner was too calm and his hands were too long-fingered and well-kept; the air of the professional gambler was clearly stamped upon him, and the men of San Lorenzo hesitated and then held back, though most people west of the Mississippi seem to regard an invitation to a card game like an invitation to a fight, something that must necessarily be accepted out of sheer manhood.

However, there was one fellow who accepted now. He was a slender young man with dark, expressive eyes, and he said: "I'll take a hand with you, stranger."

Cort looked up at him with a welcoming smile that turned almost at once into a look that was almost fear. Then he pushed back his own chair.

"Matter of fact," said he, "I forgot that I haven't time to tackle a new game. But I'll buy you a drink, stranger, and play with you some other time."

The other went with him to the bar and asked for beer, a small one.

"Still the same old Speedy, eh?" said Cort. "Nothing strong enough to make the head dizzy, eh?"

Speedy did not start. He merely said: "You remember me, Cort, do you?"

"Remember you?" said Cort. "I'd be a fool to forget the hand you dealt yourself and a few more of us in Denver, that time. After that night, I don't play with you, Speedy. I make my living out of cards. I don't aim to lose it."

Speedy raised his glass of beer and gravely regarded his companion over its foam.

"Happy days!" said he.

"And plenty of 'em," replied Cort.

They drank, and Cort went on: "The judge will be sentencing Dupray in an hour or so, Speedy," he added. "Is that why you came to town?"

"That's one reason," said Speedy. "Not that I want to hear Dupray sentenced to be hanged by the neck until he's dead, dead, dead, but I want to see what happens afterward."

"What will happen?"

"I don't know. I'm just here to look on. It's not my show, now." He shrugged his shoulders. "I'm going out into the street opposite the courthouse. Coming that way?"

"Sure," said Bill Cort.

He paid and went at once down the street with his companion, adding as they went along: "Here you are in San Lorenzo, and everybody in the town would turn out and give you a cheer if they only knew that you're the man who—"

"Forget it, will you?" pleaded Speedy.

When they came near the courthouse, Cort said: "Why don't you go inside, Speedy? Why not step in there and see Dupray take it?"

"And hear the judge sentence him to hang?" asked Speedy, with a shudder. "I couldn't do that, Bill. I haven't the nerve to stand it."

"You haven't the nerve?" exclaimed his companion. "But, great Scott, Speedy, there isn't anything in you but nerve, tons of it!"

"I couldn't stand it," repeated Speedy, firmly. "To hear one man, in a black cap, say to another: 'I condemn you to be hanged by the neck till you are dead, dead.' No, no, Bill, I couldn't stand that."

"But that devil and his gang have killed scores and scores. You know that, Speedy. You must know all about it!"

"I know a good deal about what Dupray and his people have done," said Speedy. "But it makes me sick when I think of one man standing up in cold blood and sentencing another man to be killed. It seems to me like murder, like vicious murder. Let's stand over here and see if anything happens after the sentence is pronounced."

Cort took his place beside Speedy, across the street from the little courthouse of the town. "D'you think that some of Dupray's gang may come down here and try to shoot up the crowd to get their boss away?"

"I don't know," said Speedy, his eyes absently wandering over the steady stream of men and women who were hurrying up the steps of the building.

The whole town of San Lorenzo seemed to have emptied itself up the steps of the courthouse and through its double doors. No one appeared in the street except a twelve-mule team which now entered the foot of the street and came slowly onwards, hauling a wagon with wheels as high as the head of a man. A real old-time freighter was that!

In the meantime, a hush settled over that little white town, and the quiet became so intense that finally Cort could hear out of the distance the wavering, shrill sound of a baby, crying. As the silence grew, so did the volume of that complaining sound appear to grow.

The long wait lengthened. They could hear the distant

creak and rattle of the big freighter as it drew nearer. They could watch the tall man who walked beside the near wheeler, with a blacksnake draped over his neck and one hand on the jerk-line.

He was becoming an important item in the landscape, and William Cort watched with an eye fascinated, like that of a small child on a drowsy, weary afternoon.

Then he was aware that Speedy had started suddenly and, looking down, he saw that the smaller man had actually put his hands over his ears.

His head was bowed; there was a wrinkle of pain across his forehead, and it was plain that he was suffering.

What troubled him? Only now did Cort hear, from across the street and through the wide-open double doors of the courthouse, a droning voice that came faintly to his ears.

He understood, suddenly, that that was the voice of the judge, pronouncing sentence.

Speedy had drawn back a little, so that he was resting his shoulders against the wall behind him. Still his head was bowed and his shoulders raised. He was for all the world just like a man facing a bitterly cold wind.

"It's over," said Cort, looking curiously at his companion, with a little touch of contempt in his eyes. "And right now Dupray can start getting ready to die. He'll have a lot more time to prepare for death than he's given some of his victims."

Speedy lifted his head, with an impatient light in his eyes.

"Bill," he said, "do you hold it against a mountain lion when it slaughters a calf?"

"That's the nature of the beast," said Cort. "Of course, that's different."

"Well," said Speedy, "Dupray's a beast, and that's his nature."

"Then he surely ought to die," said Cort.

"I suppose so! But I'd never lift my hand if somebody tried his rescue right here in the open street. I'd rather help him get away, I think," muttered Speedy.

"And let him go gunning for you again, afterward?" suggested the other.

"Perhaps," said Speedy. "But here they come!"

Out through the double doors of the courthouse came the throng. They were talking earnestly, nodding their heads, as though they all had heard things with which they were in perfect agreement.

But the sound of their voices could not be heard, for the twelve-mule team was close at hand now, the hoofs stamping into the dust, with a deep, muffled sound, the bells ringing above the iron-bound hames, while the great wagon lurched and rattled along behind.

In the doorway of the courthouse, when the throng had passed out, there now appeared a rather small man with a broad, round, pale face, ugly and featureless even from a distance.

"That's Dupray!" exclaimed big William Cort. "That's the frog-faced devil! I'll know him from today on, if they don't hang him as they ought to!"

About the condemned man moved no fewer than six guards, two with rifles in the rear, the others with revolvers. One pair had linked arms with Dupray, while the third pair of guards marched in front with naked guns, as though ready to charge through any attempt at rescue.

"They've got him tight enough," said Cort, pleased at the spectacle. "They'll keep him in spite of the devil and high water. Won't they, Speedy?"

"I don't know," said Speedy, shaking his head. "There are too many of them to please me."

"What's wrong with having six guards?"

"This is wrong with it," said Speedy. "Every one of the six is trusting something to the other fellow. You never can tell what will happen to a crowd, and six makes up a crowd, I'd say. I'd rather trust one proved guard than six. One guard, or maybe two, seeing that it's Dupray!"

"A couple of 'em might be carrying sawed-off shotguns, just to make sure, but otherwise everything looks hunky-dory to me," commented William Cort.

He had hardly finished speaking when there came a yell from some people who were crowding the street.

It seemed that the near mule in the lead had become caught by a snarl in the jerk-line that controlled it. At any rate, it was throwing up its head and swerving rapidly to the right, as though obeying the harsh command, "Gee!"

Swiftly it swung over, crowding the off mule of the span, with a great jingling of bells. The driver, a tall man with buck teeth, and a mirthless smile on his face, rushed forward and shouted loudly.

"That's Bones, I think," Cort remembered afterward hearing his companion murmur. "Bones! The nervy devil to come down here in broad daylight!"

In spite of the shouting of the driver, the near mule in the lead veered more and more uncontrollably. Then, as though dreading punishment from the long-legged driver, bolted to the rear.

Six spans of mules, in an instant, were curling back, scattering the crowd as if with a cavalry charge. Straight back toward the armed escort of the prisoner they rushed, and the guards, with yells to one another, started hauling Dupray back from the danger.

But the speeding line of mules came too fast. They dropped their charge and ran for their lives, while Dupray sprinted straight inside that danger and made for the wagon.

Out of it, at the same instant, there came four armed men, who closed around the escaped man and, doubling around behind the wagon, dashed across the street.

Not twenty yards from the place where Speedy and Cort were standing, they headed into the mouth of an alley that led down toward the San Lorenzo River.

Cort had pulled his own revolver, instinctively, but Speedy knocked up the muzzle of it.

"He deserves to win today," said Speedy. "Anyone who can induce that many men to risk their lives for him, certainly deserves to get away."

Into the mouth of the alley in pursuit poured the guards, now, screeching with rage, shouting orders to one another, with the whole town behind them.

"A mob," said Speedy, calmly, "and a mob will never catch Dupray."

# 32

"Lend me a hundred dollars, Bill, will you?" asked Speedy. "I have to line out as fast as I can pelt. I have a long ride ahead of me now."

"Sure," said Cort. "Two, if you want it."

"Two is better," said Speedy, "because I have to buy a mustang and a saddle and bridle. Listen to them yelping like a hunting pack, down there in the distance!"

For the hunt already had reached the edge of the river, as they could tell by the peculiar quality of the echoes that floated back through the troubled air of San Lorenzo.

"He'll get off clear," said Cort, shaking his head. "He'll get clear away. They're sure to have a fast boat waiting for him down on the water."

"Of course, they have," said Speedy. "Now they're shooting from the shore, and they wish that they had cannon instead of rifles, I suppose. But they'll never get at Dupray that way. He's beaten them. That fox has beaten 'em fair and square."

"He's beat 'em," said Cort, counting out two hundred dollars, and adding a hundred for luck.

Then he continued, anxiously: "Speedy, when I pulled this gun, I was about to take a snap shot at Dupray as he ran, and he turned his ugly frog-face and marked me with his eyes. I saw him, and I've an idea that I'll hear from him later on."

"He won't forget," agreed Speedy. "You can be sure of that. I'm sorry, Bill. But I couldn't let you shoot him down when he was one step from freedom. Besides, you might have missed. You probably would, at that distance, and shooting at a running man."

"I might have missed," muttered Bill Cort, "but he won't miss when he takes his crack at me."

"He doesn't miss," agreed Speedy. "He's one of the people who can't afford to."

"By thunder, Speedy," exclaimed Cort, sweat standing on his forehead. "I begin to feel a little nervous. What about you?"

"About me? Oh, I've got to catch him if I can. Anyway, I must try to warn some friends of mine. I've got to get the news to them as fast as I can."

"Who?"

"John Wilson. The fellow who was with me, when we caught Dupray. Dupray will want my scalp first of all now, and then he is going to want Wilson's."

"Perhaps he won't want yours at all," replied Cort. "He saw me pull a gun, and he saw you knock the gun up. That ought to wipe out all old scores."

"My score can never be wiped out," answered Speedy, unmoved. "It's too long and too black. The point is that Dupray was a great legend a month ago. Now he's been dragged out into the open sunshine. People know what he looks like. They know that he can be deceived and beaten. They'll try to catch him, now, as they never tried before."

"I suppose you're right. No gratitude in the dog, nothing but a mouthful of teeth and poison!" said Cort. "Well, Speedy, when you ride out to see the Wilsons, I've an idea that I'd like to go along."

"You?" exclaimed Speedy, surprised.

Cort nodded. "I don't want that frog-faced beast to take after me," argued the gambler. "And I'd rather be with you than with anybody else in the world, when it comes to facing Dupray. Will you take me along?"

Speedy, frowning, drew out the money he had just received and fingered it, his mood impatient.

"It's all right if you don't want me," said Cort, frankly. "I know how it is. You don't have much to do with crooks and you know that I'm a crooked gambler. Well, so is every other gambler in the world. Besides, Speedy, I'm not such a bad bargain. I can ride with most people. I can shoot a good deal better than average, a whole lot better than average. I think my nerves are pretty steady, most of the time. Only, that greasy-gray frog-face is lodged in the back of my mind, and it won't rub out. Let me ride along with you, will you?"

"Why not?" muttered Speedy, thoughtfully. "Yes, come

along, old friend, and we'll try this trail together, though I generally ride alone. Come on!''

They bought two good, seasoned mustangs, and quickly mounting, they loped the horses out of San Lorenzo.

They had the details of the escape some time before they left. Straight down to the edge of the San Lorenzo River, Dupray had been rushed by his escort, and there a boat was waiting for them, a very long, light craft.

Into that long boat the whole gang leaped and thrust her adrift. They jerked up the sail and, as they flung themselves down into the shelter of the heavy bulwarks, the wind bellied the sail, made the boat lean over, and shot it out into the stream.

A rain of rifle bullets and slugs from wide-mouthed revolvers followed, as a matter of course.

Men said that a thousand holes must have been knocked in the bottom of the little ship, as it heeled over in the wind. For all that, it did not sink, but safely turned the corner of the next river bend. The townsmen, following in swiftly paddled craft or straining at long oars, reached the bend of the river, rounded it, found the boat stranded and the crew gone, and in their ears beat the noise of pounding hoofs.

As Speedy said, when he heard the final details: ''You see how it is, Bill. In Dupray, yonder, you have a fellow with the brains of a philosopher and the heart of a grizzly bear. No! A bear is a big, warm, affectionate beast compared to that snake of a Dupray.''

''And you, Speedy,'' cried out his companion, ''you stood by and looked on, when you might have stopped him. You could have stopped him, if you'd wanted to!''

''Not after the rush began,'' argued Speedy. ''There were too many of 'em.''

''You could have done it, if your heart had been in the business,'' insisted Cort. ''Instead of that, you've turned the devil loose on the world again!''

''Not I,'' said Speedy. ''Six strong-armed guards turned him loose, when a team of mules charged 'em.''

''And now that he's free, you are in danger of your life.''

They had talked like this as they labored into the dusky, thick light of the evening, up a long slope, their horses fairly staggering beneath them, for they had ridden them out, as they approached the end of their journey.

Now, at the top of the hill, they saw a house in the hollow beyond. Lights gleamed from the windows, and Speedy murmured: "Bill, I blame myself, but I can't change myself. When I see a hunt, my heart is with the fox, not with the hunters."

# 33

"That's peaceful," said William Cort, as they rode their horses down the slope.

"It is," agreed Speedy, "but every minute now, you'd better act as though the witches were just around the corner."

"You mean, you think Dupray could get out here as soon as this?"

"I don't know," said Speedy. "Whatever we've done, he can probably do. Of course, he may decide on a few little robberies to make up for lost time before he goes after John Wilson and me. But I doubt it. I imagine that what's nearest and dearest to his heart is the thought of taking our scalps. That house looks peaceful, as you say, but for all we know, those lights down there may be shining in dead faces."

"Quit it, Speedy," said his companion, his voice half choked. "You chill my bone to the marrow."

They came up to the house through a valley road which ran, winding, through several groves of trees and so came to the house itself. As far as could be told, it was like most other ranch houses, being long and low throughout, except for one wing, which was of two stories. It had a hitching rack in front and a dim tangle of corral fencing to the rear, with a few sheds nearby and a great square-shouldered barn.

"Ranching and farming," said Speedy, pointing to a field of grain that swept up almost to the edge of the house on one side. "I didn't know that Wilson would make such a good man in the open."

He tethered his horse at the rack in front of the house, and went to the door, not in front, but in the rear, opening apparently into the kitchen. A woman's voice, singing, came out as if to welcome them on purpose.

Speedy laid a hand on the shoulder of his companion, stopping him to say: "I'd rather hear that voice than opera, Cort. A lot rather. I've been thinking of her lying in a pool of blood and that same throat cut from ear to ear. And now—"

He went on again, hastily, and knocked at the door.

"Come in!" cried out the singer, breaking off.

Speedy pushed open the door on a typical ranch kitchen, under a slanting roof, as though the shed that housed this important room had been added to the whole as an afterthought.

In the center of the room there was a long, capacious table and, near one end of it, the sink, with a big wooden draining board. It was at that end of the table that Jessica Wilson was standing, rolling out a slab of dough for biscuits. Her face was reddened from the heat; she was befloured to the bare elbows, and she dropped the rolling pin to throw up the whitened hands and clap them together.

"Speedy!" she cried, running to him.

She drew him in by both hands, released him only for an instant to greet Will Cort, and then caught at the smaller man again.

"You've come at last!" she exclaimed. "And for how long, Speedy? A month, a week, a day? Your room is upstairs, ready and waiting. We planned it specially when we built the house, you know. No one has ever slept in it. We vowed that it would be kept for you, and you've never been near us! Speedy, how long will you stay?"

"I don't know," said he. "The fact is, Jessica, that I'm just loafing across country with my friend, Cort. We're not in any great hurry. We're just drifting as the fancy moves us."

"Then let your fancy move you to stay here. There's perfect shooting. Deer, Speedy. The woods are full of deer. It's a regular preserve!"

"Never shot a deer. I'm no hunter," said Speedy.

She drew back a little and regarded him with a slight cloud on her face.

"No, Speedy," she agreed. "I forgot about that. I forgot that you don't hunt dumb animals!"

Still frowning a little, she added: "Are you on a trail now?"

"No," said he, frankly. "I'm on no man-trail, if that's what you want to know. But I've got something to talk over with John. Where is he?"

"He's out in the barn. He'll be in, in a moment. He's feeding the horses, the plow team. All the men went off today. The cook, too."

"All quit on you?"

"No, they had a day off, to celebrate. It's the anniversary of our buying of the farm, and we turned all the boys loose with a little extra money. They scooted off this morning, and they won't be back till the morning, I suppose. We're doing our celebrating by having a quiet evening alone. And now you come to make it a real party."

"I'll step out to the barn," said Speedy, "and see John. Bill, you stay with Jessica in the kitchen."

The girl looked hard at Speedy, saying: "There's something wrong; there's something important!"

"Something that would be important if I didn't get the news to John right away," said Speedy, and hurriedly left them.

Out to the barn he ran, and, pushing back the sliding door, he heard a man whistling softly, while he pitched down quantities of hay into the long row of mangers.

"It's a musical family," said Speedy gloomily to himself. "I hope that they don't have to howl for it, before long."

Then he raised his voice.

"John!" he called.

There was a shout of joyful astonishment. Then big John Wilson came climbing down a ladder from the top of the mow and grasped the hand of his friend.

Yet his first question was: "Is there anything wrong?"

"Dupray was sentenced to death, today," said Speedy, "and on the way out of the judge's court, he was rescued and taken safely away from the town."

The head of Wilson went back, and his eyes closed, as he groaned in dismay.

"That's the worst news of a lifetime!" said he. "You came out to warn me. You think that he'll take the trail for this place?"

"I more than think it," said Speedy. "There's more poison in him than in any snake. He's sure to come, John."

"I haven't a man on the place," said Wilson.

"There's yourself and me," said Speedy, "and I've brought a good fighting man along with me. I don't know how far he's to be trusted, but he'll fight."

"I have you," said Wilson, "and that's a lot more to me than to have a whole army of other men. Where's the other fellow?"

"He's at the house with Jessica."

"Have you told her?"

"No, I haven't told her yet. There's no need to torture her until the last minute."

They stood and regarded one another silently for a moment. A rising wind went softly, drearily, through the top of the haymow of the barn.

"You're getting fat and brown," said Speedy, nodding and smiling.

John Wilson made a gesture that banished such small considerations.

"We'd better get back to the house," said he.

"Yes, we'd better," said Speedy, nodding his head. "The moon's coming up; I saw the glow of it like a fire between the mountains as I came out to the barn. It's better to get back now, before—well, Dupray has men who shoot pretty straight by moonlight, even."

Wilson nodded, and moved a hand back to his hip.

"Still carrying a gun, John?" asked Speedy.

"I've formed the habit," said Wilson. "Even with Dupray in jail, I've had my worries. I've always wondered when some of the Dupray gang would turn loose on me."

"Dupray wouldn't let 'em," said Speedy.

"Wouldn't let 'em? Why not?"

"He wants to save you and me for his own handiwork. I imagine that's what's in him." He pulled back the sliding door of that side of the barn, as he spoke.

"How about you?" asked Wilson. "Still carrying no guns?"

"People who carry guns are always tempted to use 'em, sooner or later," answered Speedy, rather shortly.

They stepped out into the night, walking past the long watering troughs down the side of the corral, and toward the house, Speedy half a step in the lead, Wilson, with a high head, keeping a lookout on every side.

Yet it was Speedy who said: "Be ready to run for it. There's something yonder in that grain field—now!"

As he finished, several dark forms rose out of the grain, only their heads and shoulders looming, and guns began to chatter. The air about Wilson and Speedy was filled with sounds like the buzzing of wasp wings blown down an incredibly swift wind. The two broke into a run and shot for the house.

A very fast man was big John Wilson but, despite his length of leg, he saw Speedy drift out ahead of him. Yet the smaller man was not running straight, but wavering from side to side, like a snipe flying from danger.

It looked as if it were going to be impossible for them to gain the safety of the house, when from a back window of the place a revolver commenced barking rapidly. At the first sound of it, the shadowy forms disappeared into the grain from which they had risen.

The two fugitives reached the kitchen door. It was jerked open before them, and they ran in past the white face of Jessica Wilson.

Bill Cort was stepping back from a window in the kitchen and reloading his emptied revolver.

Cort could not help noticing that the girl made no outcry, though her first intimation of the trouble had come from the noise of the guns.

"We have four here," said Cort, "and there's moonlight to keep watch by. One of us must take, each, a side of the house and we'd better have rifles."

"That's the only thing to do," agreed Wilson. "Jessica may not do much shooting, but she can keep watch as well as any of us and give an alarm."

"It's no good," said Speedy.

"What's no good?" asked Wilson.

"It's Dupray's gang?" said Jessica, quietly.

"And Dupray with it," said Speedy. "He got away after his condemnation in court, today."

He went on, having disposed of that subject: "The house is too big to guard all four sides of it. And they can touch a match to it, and see us all go up in smoke."

All three of the others groaned.

"What's to be done then, Speedy?" asked Wilson.

"The wind is carrying from the grain field toward the house," said Speedy. "We can't backfire the ground about it, for that reason. There's nothing to be done."

"You mean that we're lost, Speedy," said the girl.

"We're lost," said Speedy.

"You mean that there's nothing for us to do," exclaimed Wilson.

"There's supper to eat," said Speedy, "and we might as well have it in here. It's warmer in here than in the dining room."

The others exchanged stony glances. But every one of them felt that a final judgment had been spoken. While there was hope, Speedy would be the man who would find the way of deliverance. When he surrendered, it meant that nothing could be attempted.

Jessica went to the stove, opened the oven door, and took out a steaming pan of biscuits. She started to lay out food on the long kitchen table, and Speedy assisted her. Wilson and Cort were too stunned to move. All the cold speculations of death were in their eyes.

Then they sat down. Wilson and Cort could not eat. But Speedy and the girl went steadily on with the meal. They talked to one another. He asked about the farm. She told him the story of it cheerfully. Good luck had followed them every moment since the capture of Dupray.

Outside the house a voice called: "Speedy! Oh, Speedy!"

Speedy lifted his head, and frowned a little with critical interest.

"Dupray's calling me," he said, and pushed back his chair.

# 34

The mere sound of the voice had made big John Wilson snatch out his revolver, saying: "It's the devil himself!"

But Jessica Wilson ran around the table, as Speedy rose, and put herself between him and the door.

"You don't mean that you'll go out to him, Speedy, do you?" she asked.

He looked at her in a strange way, as she never had been looked at before, as though she were not a young and pretty woman, as though she were not human, in fact, but merely an obstacle, and his voice was cold when he answered: "John, take charge of your wife, will you?"

"Hold on, Speedy," muttered Wilson. "Are you saying that you would go out there and face Dupray and his killers?"

"Are you both going to interfere?" asked Speedy. "I'm not saying that I'll go out to them. I'm simply saying that I'll answer Dupray. John, will you keep Jessica in hand?"

He glanced fiercely toward Wilson, and the latter laid his hand on the arm of the girl.

"Speedy knows best," said Wilson, though his face was drawn and white as he turned toward his old companion in arms.

"It's all right, John," said the girl. "I won't make a scene. I know that we can't control him; he'll do what he wants. You can take your hand away!"

Speedy already had unbolted the rear window's shutter, and now he threw a look over his shoulder.

"Put out the lamp, will you?" he commanded.

Cort stepped forward and obeyed.

Through the darkness, only the fire in the stove gleamed with a red eye, through little openings.

Then Speedy pushed the window wide open.

"Hello, Dupray!" he called.

The voice of the bandit answered, amazingly close at hand: "Glad to hear you so close, Speedy, old man."

"Thanks," said Speedy.

"I saw you today in San Lorenzo," said Dupray. "You and your new friend, Cort, the gambler."

"Yes, we saw you there," said Speedy.

"I saw him try to make the gunplay that you stopped," said Dupray. "And he's a good shot, I hear."

"He's a good shot," agreed Speedy.

"I want to know why you played me that good turn," demanded Dupray.

"My sympathy runs with the fox, not the hounds," said Speedy.

"That's a partial answer only," said Dupray. "You must have recognized Bones, driving the team, too, didn't you?"

"Yes, that was easy."

"Why didn't you give the people a warning?"

"It was the business of the law to keep you, Dupray," said Speedy. "I'd never send a man back to wait for the hangman, if I could help it."

"You're in my hand, Speedy," said the other.

"I know it," said Speedy. "You scratch a match, and the house burns."

"You have brains," said the other. "Why didn't you think the thing up before you caged yourself in the house?"

"We had to come to the two inside," said Speedy.

"Oh, loyalty, eh?" said Dupray.

Then he laughed, his voice ringing with a sneer of contempt. He added: "I'll make a bargain with you, Speedy."

"What sort?"

"There's three more beside you, in there, eh?"

"Yes, three more."

"There's Mrs. Wilson and there's her precious husband, among the rest."

"Yes, they're both here."

"Floating on the crest of the wave, they've been, eh?"

"They've been prosperous, if that's what you mean."

"They won't last prosperous," said the criminal, angry conviction in his voice. "But I'll make a bargain with you for them."

"I'm listening."

"Swear yourself in as my man for thirty days, and I'll let the lot of them go—for tonight. As long as you're working for me. I'll keep away from 'em. Does that sound to you?"

"No, no, no!" cried Jessica Wilson.

"Be still!" said Speedy shortly. He added: "That sounds all right to me. What sort of work?"

"Any work I choose to give you," said the other.

Speedy paused, and in that pause the snarling, self-satisfied laughter of Dupray began and ended. Then Dupray went on:

"I don't much care. I'd as soon close my hand over the four of you tonight and call it quits."

"The girl, too?" asked Speedy. "You wouldn't let her leave the house?"

"Let her leave, and fill the world with talk afterward? I'm not that much of a fool, Speedy. No, it would be just one of those accidental affairs. Fire catches in the grain, cause unknown. House and four souls in it burn to cinders. That's all!"

"I see your point of view," said Speedy calmly.

"You see my point of view, but what are you going to do about it?"

"If I make the bargain with you and leave the house, I trust your word and honor not to harm anything on the place."

"You trust my honor," said Dupray, laughing brutally again. "That's all that you have to trust, Speedy. The word and the honor of Charley Dupray!"

He laughed once more, for the unique idea seemed to please him.

"Well," said Speedy, "that makes a fair bargain. I take your word and step out of the house. You may shoot me down as soon as I appear and burn the house afterward. Or perhaps you only want to get your hands on me, because a quick death by bullets or fire is not exactly what you want to give me, eh?"

"That may be it," said Dupray. "You won't know. You'll simply have to take your chance. I whistle, you dog, and you've got to come and lick my hand."

"And afterward," said Speedy, "you'd trust my promise to work for you thirty days?"

"I know the kind of a fool you are, and that your word's safer than steel handcuffs on another man. Yes, I'll trust you that far."

"Very well," said Speedy, "then I'll come out."

He closed the shutters of the window and bolted them.

"Light the lamp," he said.

Cort lighted the lamp. Jessica Wilson began to cry out, sobbing wildly, her words almost undistinguishable.

Speedy was saying to her, sternly: "This is hard enough for everybody, and you're only making it harder. I know what you want to say. You want us to stay together, and all die together in the flames. But we don't choose to do that. I know that Wilson would die fighting with me; so would Cort. They're both brave men. But they see what I see. It may be that this is simply a trap set by Dupray to put his hands on me and work his pleasure. But it also may be that he means what he says, and that he really needs me for some work that's not exactly in his own line. Now, be quiet.''

She had fallen on her knees, in a paroxysm of despair, but now she stood up. So, mastering herself, she managed to say: "You're right, Speedy. You've always been right. You've saved John for me twice. Now I suppose that you'll risk your life again, but to surrender to that devil of a Dupray!''

She slipped into a chair and leaned back against the wall, suddenly, very faint.

And Speedy said: "You're worth it. You, Jessica, and you fellows, too. Besides, a man has to die sometime.''

He waved his hand, and turned abruptly to the door, saying, casually: "So long, everyone.''

He was out in the open moonlight before anyone could interfere with his movements. Turning the corner of the house, he walked straight out through the grain field.

He waded slowly through that brittle sea of brown, with the dust rising up into his face.

Then, out of the deep grain around him, half a dozen men arose, suddenly, and seized him, and the noose of a rope flung over his shoulders bound his arms tight against his sides.

Dupray stepped before him, laughing, sneering, and nodding his frog-face with delight.

"Now, you fool," he said, "you're in my hands at last. When will you get out of 'em?''

# 35

He did not wait for an answer but, turning, he led the way. The captive was to be taken behind a clump of trees and shrubbery that shielded them from the sight of the people in the house, in case that any of these should understand what was happening and undertake to interrupt the procedure with a rifle bullet.

"Here, Bones and Sid," said Dupray, after he had looked to the way in which the hands of Speedy were bound behind his back, his feet being secured, also. "You've got enough of a grudge to be useful, now. You stay here with me. The rest of you boys, spread out and watch the house. Cort's nothing much, I hear, but I know that John Wilson can put up a fight. Watch everything. If you don't like the looks, start in and shoot as much as you please. Pass the word around. I'm pleased with the whole lot of you. We've done things before, together, but nothing that I like as well as this."

They withdrew. The tall form of Bones and the stockier silhouette of Sid remained close by, while Dupray, as though excess of triumph made it impossible for him to stand still, began to walk up and down in front of his captive.

"A bright fellow, with a brain and a pair of hands, that's what you are, Speedy," said he. "But, after all, Dupray has the poison that puts you down, eh? Charley Dupray is the man to put you down. Now I can see you die. I can taste the death of you!"

He came close to Speedy and stood, swaying a little from side to side.

"You're an ugly-looking toad," said Speedy. "What more does it prove? You've got me. Go ahead and use me. I can't help myself, and you've got helpers enough. Start the music, Dupray, and watch me dance. I suppose you'll do enough to make me dance, even with my feet tied together."

"The devil!" muttered Dupray.

He stepped still closer, and peered into the face of Speedy.

"You're an actor. You're a fine actor, Speedy," said he. "Some people might think that you're not even afraid, now, of what's going to happen to you!"

"It will last a certain time, and then it'll finish," answered Speedy.

"You can do some groaning for your friends in the house, Speedy," said the other. "When the flame hits the girl—she's a regular rose of a girl, isn't she?"

"Yes, she's a pretty thing," said Speedy, calmly.

"Well, when the flame hits her, she'll die fast. It'll only be ten or fifteen minutes for her, eh?"

His eyes worked busily over the face of Speedy, as he strove to read the mind of his captive. But Speedy answered: "Yes, only ten or fifteen minutes."

"You'll be howling long before that, Speedy," said Dupray.

"I won't howl, partner," said Speedy.

"You're sure, are you?"

"I'm sure."

"I can do things that would bring the music out of a stone, I tell you!" exclaimed Dupray.

"It won't bring the music out of me," insisted Speedy.

"Damn you," said Dupray, "I'll have you screeching if I have to find your nerves one by one and tear 'em out with hot pincers."

"After you start your little game," said Speedy, "you'll never get a whisper out of me. Start in, Dupray. I've made a fool of you before this, and tonight I'll make a fool of you again."

"Will you?" said Dupray. "Why, damn you!"

He caught a deep breath, and exclaimed: "Speedy, you're iron all the way through. I thought that I'd shake you up a little before I pushed the deal through. But tell me, you mind-reading devil, you, did you guess from the first that I was only bluffing about the torture business?"

"No, I didn't guess that," said Speedy. "You mean that you honestly intend to carry out the bargain that you made with me through the window of the house?"

"I mean it. It's a bitter thing, to me, the way that I have you here in my hand, Speedy," said Dupray. "And yet I can't close my hand on you, because I need you for another job of mine."

He waved to his two men.

"Back up," said the chief, curtly.

They moved off, together, and Dupray, after staring intently at his prisoner, said: "I've got your word, Speedy?"

"You've got my word," said Speedy.

Dupray drew a knife, touched the cords, and instantly the prisoner was again a free man.

Dupray stood a pace and a half back from him. That was all.

"You know the town of Clausen?" asked Dupray.

"Yes. I know it."

"Tell me what it looks like, then."

"It's in a ravine wedged between two mountains, with a river running through its backyards. It has one good-sized plaza, and its jail is in the center of a fine lawn."

"That's it," said Dupray, "you've hit it. The scoundrels, they wouldn't build a city hall, or some such nonsense. They had to put all of their money into a fine jail, filled with tool-proof steel and such things."

"I know it," said Speedy.

"Were you ever inside that jail?"

"Yes."

"Ha!" cried Dupray. "You mean to say that you escaped from it?"

"No, not that. I was just jailed as a material witness in a little crime in a saloon. That was all. I was let out the next day, fast enough."

Dupray sighed.

"Anyway, you know the inside of the building?"

"Yes."

"Well," said Dupray, "inside of that jail, there's a special cell, made extra strong, with a door that weighs two hundred pounds on it."

"Yes?" murmured Speedy.

"And behind that door," said Dupray, "there's a nephew of mine."

"Yes?" said Speedy.

"Understand?" said Dupray, his voice growing suddenly fierce. "He's my nephew. He's my blood. He's the only blood I got in the world. He's my heir. Except for him, what would I do with my money, I ask you."

"That's a good reason for wanting him loose," said Speedy. "What's he in for?"

"Murder," said Dupray.

"Oh, murder?" said Speedy.

"That's what they say," said the other. "But everybody knows that he's my nephew. They'd say anything about him.

They'd accuse him of anything. Only, because he's a Dupray. You'd think that there was poison in the name, maybe!"

He stamped in the height of his impatience.

"They're trying him now," said Dupray. "It was going to be a pretty close race between us to see which of the pair would hang first. But I seemed to be pushing my nose under the wire first, just by a little."

"That's true," said Speedy. "Only, it's odd that I haven't heard any talk about the nephew. It's enough of a coincidence to fill the newspapers."

"You don't read the newspapers," said Dupray, bluntly.

"That's true," said Speedy. "How old is this nephew?"

"Twenty-one. If he goes, we're wiped out, because I'll never have a brat of my own. You follow me?"

"If this boy goes," agreed Speedy, "it's the last of the line of Dupray."

"Then d'you see the point I'm making?"

"I see it," said Speedy.

"What is it, then?"

"You can't help your nephew. Your face is too well known, and they're looking for you and your men every minute, every day. You're known, and I suppose that most of your best men are known too. But you think that I might have some luck in getting him out of the jail, before he's sentenced."

"You've put it in a nutshell," said Dupray.

"If I turn the trick, the Wilsons get out from under your hand, is that it?"

"For thirty days," said the other, bitterly. "John Wilson worked with you, Speedy, when you ran me into the jail. He has to sweat for it before I die. Cort tried to pistol me when I was breaking clear. He had nothing against me, personally, and he's got to sweat for that job."

"I made the deal. I'll stick to it," said Speedy. "But suppose that you say: if I fail to get the boy loose, in the thirty days, you go after everybody. If I succeed, then you forget about 'em, and go after me with knives and guns and as many men as you please. Will that suit you?"

Dupray, through a moment of silence, stared at the other. Then, slowly, he nodded his head. "You beat me, Speedy," he said, "but then, you're only a freak. You're not like other people. I'll make that deal with you. If you get Al Dupray free, then everything is called off, except between you and me.''

"Yes," said Speedy, "that can't be called off till one of us is dead."

"Good," said Dupray, nodding his round head again. "Now about getting you to Clausen and giving you all the help that I can."

Speedy raised his hand.

"I work alone," said he. "Even if I'm working for you, I wouldn't have your help!"

# 36

Osgood had been deputy sheriff in the town of Clausen for six months, and he was maintained in his post by the force of public opinion. "Stew," as he was nicknamed, was a big young man with rather a brutal face but, as a matter of fact, he was both good-natured and charitable, except when he saw a chance for a fight and, above all, when the fighting was with guns. Therefore, he was exactly inside the tradition of the officers who had enforced the law in the town of Clausen for the last half dozen years.

The people of Clausen were a hardy lot and they endured a long list of riots and gunfights before they decided to take a hand. The town built a fine, handsome jail with walls of solid stone. When the jail was built, Clausen elected good officials to see that the jail was kept filled, and after a few years the town became one of the most unpopular places in the world for traveling criminals.

The present sheriff of the county was now flat on his back in the hospital recovering gradually from the effects of a bullet that a certain cattle rustler had put through his body. Deputy Sheriff Stew Osgood had the place in hand, and he proved his capacity at once by going out and getting that same rustler with an accurate rifle. So Stew remained sole occupant of the sheriff's place of importance.

At this moment, Stew Osgood had turned from the bar of the White Wizard Saloon and was saying: "Look here, Mexico, you've been chasing me around all day. Whacha want anyway?"

"Job, señor," said the other.

As he spoke, he took off his tattered straw hat and showed more clearly a young face that would have been strikingly handsome, but for a long, ragged scar that puckered one cheek.

He stood bowing before the deputy sheriff.

The latter surveyed him with a mixture of contempt and amusement.

"He knows you're a big man in town, Stew," said the bartender. "That's why he's chasing you around."

"Where could I give anybody a job except over in the jail?" demanded Stew Osgood, with irritation. "We need a kind of a janitor over there. And a fine thing this would be to have in the jail, wouldn't it?"

"Looks like a mountain lion must've clawed him in the sweet days gone by," said the bartender.

"He's all gummed up," observed the deputy sheriff. "I'll bet that he ain't et a square meal in three days."

The man with the scar, who had stood before the pair as though he were incapable of understanding the words, now brightened, and bowed several times, rapidly.

*"Si, señor; si, señor!"* he murmured.

"Here's a dollar, anyway," said Stew Osgood, reaching into his pocket.

The man with the scar beamed with a crooked smile and started his bowing all over again. But now a heavy voice from the corner of the barroom boomed out: "That's why the country's goin' to hell."

"Hold on," said the sheriff. "Why is it goin' that way, brother?"

A mighty youth arose from a little corner table where he had been sipping beer.

"Why should money be throwed away on foreign dogs?" he demanded. "I'd like to know, when there's a lot of honest men of our own that ain't got a job."

"Honest men like who?" asked the sheriff.

"Like me," said the young giant, jabbing a grimy thumb against his breast by way of further identification.

Stew Osgood started to frown, for there was always plenty of battle-spirit in him. However, he controlled himself, and a wicked thought gleamed in his eye.

"I promised a dollar to somebody," said he, and flicked the broad-faced coin suddenly high in the air.

It hung spinning close to the ceiling for an instant, and then began its descent straight over the heads of the big tramp and the man of the scar.

"Out of the way, runt," said the larger of the pair, and reached up one hand for the dollar, while with the other he swung heavily at the man of the scar.

The latter avoided the swinging fist, slid in close, and with a dexterous pressure of his knee against the leg of the giant, caused the latter to sag suddenly and miss his target.

The big silver dollar fell with a resounding spat into the palm of Mexico.

At this the deputy sheriff exclaimed aloud with pleasure and surprise. "Pretty slick!" he cried out. "Pretty neat, Mexico. What happened to you, brother?"

"The dirty hound, he played a trick on me," said the tramp. "I gotta mind to eat him."

"Have you?" chuckled the deputy sheriff. "I dunno that you could, though."

Then he smiled and added: "Here's another dollar for the man that can jump the highest."

He threw a dollar into the air, but the tramp, with a string of oaths twisting out of his snarling mouth, rushed in to batter Mexico to a pulp.

The latter drew back a little and then waited, with alertness in his poise and calm in his eyes.

Only at the very last minute, he bowed his body. As he stooped, his incredibly swift hands caught an outflung arm of the tramp and, twisting himself about, he bore down with a mighty leverage.

The inevitable happened. The hulk of the tramp shot off his feet and, hurtling over the shoulder of the smaller man, it seemed as though he were purposely diving against the wall of the saloon, which he struck with a great crash.

He fell back, with a soft, thick thud upon the floor, while the man of the scar calmly picked up his dollar.

The deputy sheriff was much astonished.

"How'd he do that, Jerry?" he demanded of the bartender. "Go and throw some water on that bum and roll him out into the street, unless he's got some broken bones."

The tramp did not need the water, however. Picking himself up, he cast dizzy but wrathful glances around him, then staggered out through the swinging doors of the saloon.

"How'd you do that, Mexico?" the deputy sheriff repeated.

Mexico could only answer with a little dumb show of hands and attitudes.

The deputy sheriff looked him over again.

"You ain't much to fill the eye," said he, "but you kind of handle yourself all right, I gotta say. I gotta admit that about you. How cheap you work, son?"

A broad, smiling gesture, made with both arms, the palms of the hands up, indicated that money was no consideration, and that the honor of serving the deputy sheriff was all that he demanded.

Stew Osgood grunted.

"We gotta have somebody to tidy up around in the jail. I don't know why the kid wouldn't do. Hey, what's your name?"

"I Pedro, señor," said the other.

"You Pedro, eh?" repeated the deputy sheriff. "Well, Pedro, you be a good boy over there in the jail, and everything'll be fine for you, but if you try any tricks, I'm gonna skin you alive. Savvy!"

"Ah, señor!" said Pedro, between sadness and a smile of deprecation, as though such a possibility was forever beyond his thoughts.

# 37

The deputy sheriff had been having a drink in Jerry's saloon because, when he returned to the jail, he knew that a very unpleasant task was waiting for him.

Al Dupray was getting the third degree, and he had been getting it for the last hour, now.

The idea of Stew Osgood was simply to keep his man awake for thirty-six hours and try, by the steady pressure of questions, to make him confess a crime which, Osgood was confident, he had committed.

It was not the sort of thing that Osgood liked, but he had been told that it had to be done. The case was clear and strong against Dupray. There was hardly a doubt that he would be convicted when the case went to trial. But it would cost the county a great deal to prosecute. For the unlucky news had come in that the terrible Charles Dupray, the uncle of Al, was again free and roving. He would be certain to pour huge sums of money into the defense and, when he did that, it meant that he could hire some of the best lawyers in the country to fight out the case.

There was one way to preclude all the expense of time and dollars, and that was to secure a confession from Al Dupray. A day and a half before, the questioning had started. Now it was about to end, and Deputy Stew Osgood had prepared himself to put on the final pressure.

He strode back to the jail, with the shorter-stepping Pedro hurrying behind him.

When they got to the jail, the mind of the deputy sheriff was not upon his new employee but upon the disagreeable work before him. He simply picked a cap off a nail on the wall and jammed it on the head of Mexico. He picked off a uniform coat and threw it toward him.

"There's your outfit that shows you belong to the jail," he observed. "Now get busy. Grab a broom and a mop or something and start tidying up, Mexico."

Pedro accepted the broom as though it were the sword conferring knighthood upon him. And the deputy sheriff hurried on toward his own office.

He opened the door and stepped into a thick atmosphere of cigarette smoke. Through that mist he saw two hollow-eyed men, one upon either side of a figure that slumped down in a chair between them. The hands of Al Dupray were manacled together, being chained around one arm of the chair. Just as the deputy opened the door, one of the questioners shook

Dupray violently by the arm, and he raised his head with a start out of the instant of slumber into which he had fallen.

"You killed Tom Older," croaked the questioner who had shaken the young man by the shoulder. "Why don't you tell the truth?"

The answer was mere silence. Gloomily, the man looked up at the deputy, who scowled back in return.

"We've got you at last, kid," Osgood said.

"Have you?" muttered Dupray, looking up with hollow eyes.

"Yeah. We've got you," said the deputy sheriff. "We got your fingerprints. It don't make no difference, now, whether you confess to us or not. We got your fingerprints, all right."

"On what?" asked the young man, frowning.

"You know on what, all right," said Osgood. "We got 'em, and that winds up the case."

"What would my fingerprints be on?" asked Dupray.

"On the handle of the ax that brained poor Tom Older!" cried the deputy.

Dupray merely shook his head.

"I used that ax, but I used it to chop wood," he insisted. "That's all!" And his chin fell upon his breast; in an instant he was snoring, open mouthed.

The deputy sheriff looked at the pair.

"You been at him all the time?" he muttered.

"All the time," said one of the men. "And a hell of a dirty job it is, too."

"It's a rotten job. I hate it like you do," agreed Osgood. "But it's orders, and we've got to do what we're told. There ain't any doubt that he's the murderer, is there?"

"No," admitted one of the tormentors.

"Then," said Osgood, "it don't make much difference what we do to him. Wake him up!"

They shook him from either side. He opened his eyes with a groan of agony; but he set his teeth at once to shut off complaint and weakness.

"I've got the whole story that'll hang you," declared Osgood.

"You lie," said Dupray wearily.

"I lie, do I?" exclaimed Osgood, pretending to be in a rage. Then he made himself laugh loudly.

"We've got it hung on you at last," said he.

"You lie again."

"Do I? Here it is, all wrote out. This is the confession that you can sign, brother, and then go to bed and have a good sleep."

"I won't sign nothing," said Al Dupray.

"You're a fool if you don't sign this," said Stew Osgood. "Listen. We got all the facts, here. I leave out the beginning. I cut right into the middle. You're supposed to be talking. And this is what you'd say, if you'd tell the truth."

He began to read aloud:

" 'I kept telling Tom Older that it was no good prospecting the Clausen Hills anymore, because they'd been gone over with a fine-toothed comb for years. But he kept right on. I pointed out to him that I'd paid for the grubstake, and that I was doing my share of the camp work, too. I was sick of it, and I wanted to try some new ground, where we'd have a chance. But the fool kept right on. Finally, one night in the hills, it came to a showdown, and I told him that I wouldn't stand it any longer.

" 'He told me I could get out, if I didn't like his way of prospecting. I said I'd get out, willing enough, if he'd pay me back the grubstake money that I'd spent. He damned me for that and laughed in my face. He was as mean as a rat. That's what he looked like, an old rat. I couldn't stand it. Something exploded in my mind. I'd been cutting wood for the fire, and I still had the ax in my hand. I gave it a swing and brought it down on his head. He fell on his face. He never moved after I hit him.' "

Osgood stopped reading. "There you are, brother," he said. "All that you have to do is to sign."

"By thunder," said the prisoner, hoarsely, "it's almost straight, every line of it!"

The sheriff started violently. But he covered up his surprise by exclaiming: "Sure, it's true. We've got everything on you!"

"It's almost true, every word of it," said Dupray, still astonished. "It's true that I stood there with a load of wood in one arm, and the ax in my other hand. It's true that I cursed him for an old fool and asked him how many more days we were going to stay there among the rocks and the brush. Then he told me that we'd stay there as long as pleased him, and that he was kind of sorry that he was going to make a worthless, complaining fool like me a rich man.

"When I heard him say that, I was so mad that I heaved up the ax and said that I had half a mind to brain him with it. I did have half a mind to do it. But I recollected soon enough Uncle Charley. He always comes pop into my head, whenever I get a crazy wish to do something wrong. So I threw the ax away, and I went running off into the night, half crazy. That's the true story. That's the whole story. When I come back, there was Tom Older lying dead, and the ax was there with the blood on it, and the trail of a man that had come out of the brush to the fire, and gone away again."

"That was the trail of Pete Simmons, that came along and found the old man lying dead," declared Osgood. "Are you trying to put the blame on an honest man like Simmons? Dupray, you dog, you murdered the old man; and then you went sneaking off. It was only later that you changed your mind and came back to bluff the job out."

"Ain't Simmons staked out the mine that Tom Older found?" shouted the prisoner. "Ain't that a fact? Why wouldn't he've killed Tom, and come rushin' down to Clausen to put the blame for the killing on me and to file his claim? That's what I wanta know."

Osgood looked with sudden weariness and disgust at the wild, white face and the red-rimmed eyes.

Then he said, tersely: "Take him away and slam him into the cell again. I've done my best, but the fool won't listen to reason!"

# 38

The two third-degree tormentors jerked open the door of the sheriff's office and thrust the prisoner in willingly enough, for they hated the dirty work of the long inquisition almost as much as Al Dupray could have hated it.

As they entered the inner corridor, they almost fell over the form of the newly hired janitor, who was down on his knees, industriously scrubbing the floor just outside the door of the sheriff's office.

The two guards, looking down at the uniform coat and cap, grunted out a few oaths and went on down the hall to the aisle that led between the rows of cells.

Ten men were in those cells that night, for the deputy sheriff kept himself well occupied in Clausen, and saw to it that crime was kept in check.

They pressed against the bars of their cells and looked steadily at the accused murderer, as he passed down toward his own strong place of keeping. They could hear the clanking of the heavy chains that were fastened on him, thus fastening him to the huge steel bolts that were worked into the wall of the prison. Then they could hear the voice of one of the guards, saying, rather too loudly: "Look ahere, kid, you oughta have more sense. It ain't gonna buy you nothing, to keep your face shut, and lie like this. Everybody knows that you croaked Tom Older. You're gonna hang for it, all right."

"I know that I'm going to hang," said the young man, "but I won't put the rope around my own neck, maybe."

"You're a fool, and the biggest fool that I ever heard of," said the guard. "There you are, locked up safe and sound. Stay there and rot, till they come and get you for the rope!"

The guards walked out, the door was closed behind them, and the three keys were turned in the three locks.

They disappeared. The two larger lights were put out. And there remained only two small, flickering night lamps, to illumine the interior of the jail. They threw into every cell only a confused blur of shadows and faint light, and the eye could make out almost nothing.

Now, down the corridor, came the form of Pedro, the new janitor's assistant, with a bucket of soapy water, a scrubbing brush and a mop. He fell upon his knees, at the end of the aisle, and began to work.

A few of the prisoners went to the bars of their cells and, looking out, they scoffed at and reproached the solemn, industrious worker. One of them summed up the opinion of the others.

"What's the good of bein' a free man, if you're gonna work in a jail, kid? You might as well be doin' time yourself!"

Pedro returned no answer. He continued to scrub so patiently and so hard that his whole body shook with his movements.

Finally, the others turned in on their cots. One or two called good nights to companions up and down the aisle; but by degrees the voices died out, and soft sounds of snoring rose.

Pedro, by this time, had carried his careful scrubbing as far as the door of the cell of Al Dupray.

Now he kneeled before the door of the cell.

In his fingers appeared a thin length of steel spring, such as might have come out of the mechanism of a big watch or a clock. With this he began to fumble at the lowest and largest of the locks. Deftly he worked, his ear pressed close to the keyhole, his whole body tense with the effort of perfect concentration.

A number of minutes passed. Then there was a slight but rather prolonged sliding sound. Pedro drew back, and nodded his head with satisfaction.

Across the aisle, behind him, a voice said, quietly: "Fine, kid! You done that, pretty good. Before you open the next one, you might take a look at my door and see what you can do with it."

Pedro turned his head. He could see the dim silhouette of the prisoner, the pale gleam of the hands that clasped the bars of the cell.

He said nothing, but waited.

There was no more snoring and, looking up and down the aisle, he made out other forms, other hands. A voice said, farther away: "I'll be in on this, or I'll be damned!" And another: "We all walk out together." Pedro listened and sighed.

"Me first," said the man across the aisle, who had spoken first, "or else I'm gonna squeal. I'm gonna raise hell, I tell you! Unless you come over here, and open this door! You're a beauty, and you can use some of your good looks on me."

The man with the scar stood up from his work and turned.

How did it happen that noiseless work had awakened the prisoners?

Well, there are other mysteries of instinct, never so well exemplified as inside the walls of a prison!

Some electric current of sympathy had informed them all that what they wished for themselves was being brought to pass for another, a companion; and that one, the man of the strong room!

Then said Pedro, in perfectly good English: "Boys, will you listen to me?"

It was a very soft and quiet voice, and it was so exquisitely gauged that it barely carried to the farther end of the row of cells.

"We'll listen," said someone, halfway up the aisle and in a voice pitched like that of the speaker.

"I'm here for Al Dupray. He's here for murder," said Pedro. "And the murder he's here for is a job he didn't do. He's being railroaded because he really didn't do the job that he's accused of. Pete Simmons murdered Tom Older, and Pete threw the blame where people would believe that it ought to rest. None of the rest of you has any such charge hanging over his head. Most of you are in for small things. Let me get Dupray out of his cell, and I'll turn in and try to help the rest of you if there's time. Is that fair?"

"Fair or not," said the man across the aisle, more loudly, "you start working on my door right now, or I'm gonna raise a holler. You hear me, buddy?"

"I hear you talk," said Pedro, slowly. "I don't want to believe what I hear, though. You fellows don't think that I can empty the whole jail, do you? In less than ten minutes, there'll be a guard walking on the rounds!"

"Guard or no guard," said the man across the aisle, "you open this lock, Mr. Slick, or I holler. You can count to ten. Or I'll do the counting myself."

The new janitor paused before answering, and both his hands contracted.

Then a voice spoke, the same soft voice that had spoken before, halfway up the aisle:

"Buck?"

"I hear you, Slim," said the man across the aisle.

"Buck," said Slim, "you shut up and let the kid go on with his work. If he's got a chance, he'll turn Dupray loose and come back for the rest of us. What we got ahead of us? Maybe thirty days. No more'n that. Thirty days and it's the rope for Dupray, unless he gets loose right pronto."

"You do your own thinkin'," said Buck. "I'll think for myself and do for myself, from now on."

There was a moment of silence. The man of the scar did not speak. Neither did any of the other men in the cells up and down the aisle.

Then the voice of Slim struck in again.

"Buck, if you carry on, I'm gonna get hold of you, after I get out of this here jail. I'm gonna follow you and cut your rat's throat!"

He spoke as softly as ever. But there was all the sincerity of a prayer in his speaking.

No one broke in, but all waited and, while they waited, they counted seconds, Pedro and all the others within hearing distance. Two, three, four, five, ten counts, and then it became fairly certain that Buck was considering seriously what Slim had said.

Then the voice of Slim went on as quietly and gently as ever: "I'm Slim Malone. The one that peeps, I'm gonna remember, and I'm gonna write him down in red. You hear me? Leave the kid a free road. Leave him be!"

Still, for another instant, Pedro waited. There was no sound and, dropping again upon his knees, he fell to work upon the central lock of the three. Presently the slight sliding sound came again, and it was clear that the second lock had been mastered.

He rose to his feet and began on the third and last lock. As he did so, he was aware of something like a warning whisper, not so much heard, as felt.

He turned and saw that every man had disappeared from the bars of the cells, and down the aisle walked a guard, keys in one hand, a lantern in the other!

# 39

The new janitor removed from his hand the little bit of spring with which he was working—it had that instant turned the bolt of the lock! In its place appeared a rag of cloth, with which he started polishing the outer edge of the door.

It seemed that he had conjured the bit of rag out of the thin air. Intently he worked but, aware of the approaching steps, and aware, also, of eyes that watched him intently, like the eyes of hunted things, suffering and hoping for a fellow being, when a beast of prey is stalking.

A great hand fell suddenly upon the shoulder of Pedro. He turned his head with a sudden start and a gasp.

"Ah, señor!" he exclaimed.

The great hand lifted him to his feet. He stood agape, the pull of the scar drawing his mouth all awry.

"What's the hell's work you're doing here?" asked the guard.

"Me? Señor, I scrub, I polish all day long. I do it everything right, no?"

The guard scowled fiercely down at him. "It ain't for nothin' that I had a pricklin' in my bones," said he. "You skunk, you're up to something. What you been tryin' on those locks?"

"Señor, and what should poor Pedro try?" said the new janitor.

He clasped his hands together and looked with infinite and trembling appeal at the other.

The guard drew back a little, his scowl as black as ever, his brows drawn down in a deep shadow over his eyes.

"By the looks of you," he declared, "you ain't nothin' at all. But I ain't one to go by the looks, only. Lemme try the key on one of those locks and see if there's been any funny business, around here. That's all that I wanta see!"

He gritted his teeth in the very premonition of rage as he

spoke and, stepping forward, he knocked Pedro back and out of his way with a gesture of his hand.

It seemed to the new janitor, that the burning of the eyes from the shadow grew fiercer every moment.

The guard, in the meantime, had fitted one of the keys into the central lock, stooping to do so. As he turned the key, finding that nothing resisted against its pressure, he exclaimed suddenly under his breath.

At that moment, Pedro, moving forward on a noiseless foot, struck with the edge of his palm across the back of the guard's neck.

The man slumped to the floor.

Up and down the corridor came a sigh like the whisper of wind through an opened door.

The man of the scar paid no heed to it. He knew that it was the sympathetic intake of breath by all of those who covertly and so intensely looked out upon his doings.

He regarded not the fallen guard for the moment. It was as though he knew perfectly how long that man would lie still, benumbed by the impact of the blow, for Pedro now ran lightly as a shadow down the aisle between the cells and passed the bunch of keys through the bars into the cell of Slim Malone.

"All right, Slim," he whispered. "You can reach your hand through, and get at the lock of your door. Don't let the keys jingle. Keep on trying till you find the right one. I'm in a hurry."

He was back at the door of Al Dupray's cell instantly and pulled it open. Then he caught the limp form of the guard under the pits of the arms, dragged him inside, into the darkness, and let him slump to the floor.

Al Dupray had long since risen from his cot; he moved now, with a slight jingling of steel upon steel.

The man of the scar stepped out into the aisle again, brought in the lantern of the fallen guard, and set it on the floor.

Then he set to work upon the three locks that secured the fetters of the prisoner. As he worked, he spoke, in a voice hardly louder than a whisper.

"Your uncle sent me up to you. I'm Speedy. We made a

deal for you. I'm to work to get you free. He's to leave some friends of mine alone. That's all. If we can get out of the jail, I have horses cached."

The first lock, which was upon the hands, now yielded.

At the same time, there was a loud knocking at the front door of the jail, and Speedy leaped to his feet with a muffled exclamation.

Only for a moment he hesitated, then he said: "I'll be back. Take charge of this!"

He hauled the breathing, but still senseless guard within the grip of Al Dupray's hands, then turned and fled down the corridor between the cells.

As he passed the cell of Slim Malone, he could see the hands of the man protruding through the bars, while he patiently but clumsily tried key after key in the lock. No key, so far, had fitted!

Like a ghost, soundless, Speedy reached the door of the jail. He pushed back the complicated bolts and opened it a fraction of an inch.

"Who's there?" he asked.

"Telegram, mister," said the voice of a drawling, sleepy boy.

Speedy pulled the door open, took the telegram from the freckle-faced lad, and scrawled a word on the receipt book. Then he closed the door and, as he closed it, already his supple fingers were preparing to rip the envelope open, when he heard another door open and a brighter shaft of light shone into the hall.

It was Deputy Sheriff Stewart Osgood, saying loudly, sternly: "What's going on here?"

The man of the scar began his bowing, as he approached.

"A message for you, señor, that has come!"

He delivered it into the hands of Stew Osgood with another bow.

"Who told you to be moochin' around here at this time of night?" asked Osgood sourly. "Go on and get out of here, will you?"

"I go, señor, with thanks," said Speedy. "I go as quickly as my feet will take me. Señor is to Pedro as a father."

"You talk like a fool," said the deputy sheriff, bluntly. "Go on and get!"

He passed through the door of his office, and closed the door behind him, while Speedy turned and raced back to the open door of the cell of Dupray. Inside, there was a faint sound of scuffling and the subdued, terrible voice of Dupray, saying to the now conscious guard: "Try that ag'in, and I'm certainly gonna throttle you!"

Speedy dropped to his knees, and resumed the work that he had left off.

The second lock gave way under the magic of his small bit of wire. The third was more difficult. A fine perspiration broke out on his forehead, and began to stream down his face. He had to wink his eyes to keep the stinging sweat out of them.

Dupray, just above his shoulder, was whispering: "You're the gamest that I ever seen. I don't hardly care what happens to me, after I seen a thing like this, is all I gotta say!"

The third lock yielded, and Dupray stepped free from the shackles.

"Now this?" he asked, gesturing toward the prostrate body of the guard, and setting his jaw savagely.

"Choke him," said Speedy calmly.

"I'll do it," said Dupray, bending over, his fingers already extending like the talons of a bird.

"Don't do it, fellows," said the guard, in a voice that was a cross between whimper and whisper. "I won't make a sound. I'll lay here like I was dead. Don't bump me off, boys. I ain't gonna do a thing to give you away."

"He lies," said young Dupray, sternly. "He's a sneak, and all sneaks will lie!"

"Let him go," said Speedy. "We'll at least keep our hands clean, this far."

In the meantime, the deputy sheriff had taken the telegram into his office and was in no hurry to open it. He first made himself comfortable in his chair. Then he hoisted his heels to the edge of his desk, and he lighted a cigar. When all this had been achieved, he at last opened the missive.

Deputy Sheriff Stewart Osgood:
Word just received that Harrison Williams, alias the

Doctor, alias the Slip, alias Speedy, has undertaken to try
to free Al Dupray. Informant William Cort. Be on guard.
Disguise of Speedy often Mexican peon with scarred face.

The deputy sheriff, as he came to this portion of his long
telegram, felt his eyes thrust out from his head. He rose from
his chair, his whole body stiffening.

Speedy!

He had heard that name, a name of magic. But Speedy was
supposed to be the grand enemy of the terrible Charley
Dupray. Speedy had caught the outlaw; Speedy had clamped
him in jail, there to await the due processes of the law.

Yet, this same man was here, in that building, disguised as
the Mexican peon with the scarred face!

He caught up a revolver.

That choice he changed for a sawed-off shotgun and lurched
for the door of his office.


# 40


Down the inner corridor of the cells, Speedy and Al Dupray
had hardly started moving, when Slim Malone turned a key
that opened his door, and stepped out into the hallway. As he
appeared, with Speedy and Dupray moving rapidly down the
corridor, it became apparent to those hungry-eyed watchers in
the other cells that they had little chance of being liberated.
Now, also, the injured guard in the cell where Dupray had
been confined groaned heavily. It was like a signal. From
every throat of every prisoner in every cell there rose a howl
of rage and envy; and Buck, in particular, leaped up and
down like a baboon, screeching and shaking the bars of his
cell like an animal.

It was just as the deputy sheriff opened the door of his
office that this howling chorus arose and beat like a heavy
wave against his brain.

He looked wildly up and down, as Slim Malone fitted the

largest of the keys in the bunch into the lock of the side door of the building.

Three men were there, and plainly the deputy distinguished among them the slender outlines of his man of the scarred face.

Speedy!

He jerked up the gun and fired as the door swung open. He could have sworn that he heard the impact of the bullet as it struck flesh; but then all three were swept through the door; it slammed heavily behind them and the spring lock clanked home. Direct pursuit on that side of the jail was impossible.

Blinded with rage and with fear, feeling that his whole reputation was hanging on their escape, the deputy raced through the front door of the jail, shouting as he ran.

Down the corridor behind him came the guard, so recently stretched prostrate in the cell of Dupray.

But, as the two ran out into the open of the night, they heard the rattling hoofs of horses at full gallop, and guessed shrewdly enough that their quarry was off to a running start.

The deputy came to a halt. Sudden pursuit would hardly gain anything for the law. As he ran his eye over the ragged outlines of the mountains, he realized that there were ten thousand possible hiding places for the fugitives, one as good as the other.

There was no chance of locating them, then, unless he could read the subtle mind of the celebrated Speedy.

He could hit upon only one suggestion, and that was the house of Pete Simmons, several miles out of the town.

Again and again, Al Dupray tried to shift the blame for the killing of Tom Older upon Simmons, who was the man, in fact, who had profited by that strike which Older had made just before his death.

The story was amusing, in spite of its dreadful aftermath. Sam Deacon, riding through the Clausen Hills, had come upon Tom Older making the camp which proved to be his last and, dismounting to talk with the veteran prospector, Older had told him, with grim amusement, about the furious discontent of his young companion, Al Dupray.

"Al's ready to kill me," said Tom Older, as Sam Deacon had testified in the courtroom at the trial. "Al's ready to do me up. He says that I'm a fool to play around here where every inch has been prospected a hundred times over. He don't know that I've got this in my pocket!''

As he spoke, he had pulled out a stone chip, and showed it to the excited eyes of Deacon, with a bright veining of yellow plainly to be seen! So much was known from Sam Deacon.

But Pete Simmons, when he found the dead man and found the chip of stone in his pocket, actually located the rock from which the chip had been taken. That was why a score of men were now moiling and toiling under his direction and in his interest. He bade fair to become a rich man, as a result of that discovery of his!

At any rate, Pete Simmons was an object of hatred to Al Dupray, perhaps simply because the man had taken up the claim that might have belonged to him and to the dead man. Whatever the reasons, it well might be, no matter where the other two went, that Dupray would hunt for Simmons; one murder leads to another, the deputy sheriff was sure. And so he said to the panting guard beside him: "What happened?"

"I seen him working at the lock of the door of Dupray. The Mexican, I mean. I seen him working, and he said he was only scrubbing down the steel. I didn't think that the steel needed no scrubbing. I wondered if the fool had been tryin' to pick the locks, maybe? Anyway, I put a key in and, sure enough, the bolt had been slipped already! Just as I was about to turn and grab him, he socked me with something. I dunno what. It felt like an ax with a dull edge. My neck was pretty near broke."

"That's enough yammering," said the deputy. "Get Collins and Bill Wade. Get Thayer, too, and Millmarch. Tell them to be here in five minutes with their horses and guns. You be on hand, too. We're going to ride, tonight, and there may be some fighting at the far end of the ride, too!''

# 41

The house of Pete Simmons was a small shack that stood up high on the side of a hill, with a little rickety veranda built across the front of it.

But there was nothing small about Simmons. He was a big, burly, red-headed fellow with a loud, brawling laugh, considered good company on the range, an excellent shot, a great hunter of deer. He had a little patch of ground which was of no great use to him, and he made his money, or had made it until recently, by hiring out as a cowpuncher or as a worker in the mines.

Now, however, that he was taking gold out of the hard ground of the Clausen Hills and seemed certain of becoming a rich man before long, he had not changed his mode of living in the least. He remained where he had always been and seemed rather uninterested in the luck he was having with the mine. This caused the entire countryside to respect him more than ever.

On this night, he sat on his veranda, talking to a person who was none other than the editor of the Clausen *News* and giving forth his ideas on many things, while the editor took notes.

They had an audience of three, who had come upon them, unseen and unknown, by riding to the top of the hill behind the house and so slipping silently down to the side of the veranda. There they crouched in the brush and listened to the voices close over their heads.

The editor was about to leave.

"The main thing, Simmons," said he, "is this talk going around about you building a memorial to Tom Older. What about that? That's news that's worth the front page, and a lot of it, too!"

"You see," said Simmons, "it's this way. That mine ain't belonging to me, except you might say by clean accident. It was accident that I come across poor old Tom lyin' dead. It was a lot more of an accident that I happened to look in his pocket and found the chip of rock. You know, I was looking for something that might kind of explain why anybody would have done dirt to Older. And it was a third accident that I happened to stumble right onto the boulder that the chip had been taken off of! By rights, Older should've had that mine, him and the young fellow that murdered him. But Older ain't got any relations to claim his share of it. And I guess that Dupray's claim ain't worth a doggone. What am I to do? Put all the money into my pocket like a hog? No. I wanta do something about it and I figger that the best way is to put up something for Clausen that'll be worth while. Maybe a hospital. Maybe a courthouse, with the name of Tom Older onto it. Understand?''

"That's mighty public-spirited," said the editor. "Twenty-five thousand is a lot of thousands. But it don't look so big in print. Suppose that I push it up a little bigger and say that you're planning a fine courthouse, and that the cost would be around a hundred thousand. That'll give people something to look at and something to talk about, and it'll make you a great man in Clausen."

"Aw, you handle it the way you think is the best," said Simmons. "Go ahead and do what you please, partner."

They came clumping down the front steps, and walked down the path to the gate, beyond which was the horse and buggy of the editor. There were more agreeable messages, more good-nights, and then the newspaperman drove back up the little winding trail toward Clausen.

Big Pete Simmons remained for a moment to admire the moon and the stars. His hands were deep in his pockets and his head thrown far back, as he strolled slowly up the path, and, therefore, did not see the danger until it was just upon him. On either side of him a revolver gleamed, and three men arose out of the shadows of the brush.

Simmons said, calmly: "What you want, boys? Money? I'll give you what I've got in the house, if that's it!"

"Stick 'em up!" said Al Dupray.

The voice staggered Simmons like the blow of a bullet over the heart. He breathed a curse.

"Up with your hands!" repeated Al Dupray, through his teeth.

The hands of Simmons went swiftly up in the air. He rose on tiptoe, in his eagerness to grasp at the stars, as it seemed. "Just walk up the stairs," said Speedy, "and inside the house, Simmons. This'll soon be over. Don't be nervous. I don't think that we'll have to do anything to you. Just a minute, first."

Deftly, he picked a long-barreled Colt and a big knife out of the clothes of the other, and then Simmons walked awkwardly up the stairs, still holding his hands stiff and high above his head.

He had to lower them a little, going through the front door of the house. Now they gathered in the small front room, where the long arms of Simmons kept the tips of his fingers touching the ceiling.

He was pale, but his face was grimly set rather than unnerved and sagging from overmastering fear.

"Sit down, sit down," said Speedy, taking quiet control of the situation. "Sit down, Simmons, and we'll have a little chat together."

"All right," said Simmons.

He drew in a breath as he lowered his arms, and then pulled up a chair to the table.

"I'd like to finish him off, right now," said Al Dupray suddenly. "Speedy, give him his gun, and let the two of us have it out!"

"Speedy?" exclaimed Simmons. "Are you Speedy?"

"Some people call me by that name," answered Speedy.

"Well," sighed Simmons, "I'm glad of that. You're never mixed up with crooked work. Speedy, what's the deal about?"

"It's about the way you murdered Tom Older and laid the blame on Dupray," replied Speedy.

The shock made Simmons close his eyes. When he opened them they were dark with desperation.

"Is that the kind of a gag that they've talked over to you, Speedy?" he complained.

"That's the gag," said Speedy. "We've got the information, Simmons, but we want your signed confession before we send you to the jail."

"Signed confession?" said Simmons, growing more and more colorless.

He looked wildly about him, toward the two faded photographs of his father and mother that hung on the wall. He seemed to study the details of the tattered wallpaper, also; and then he looked down to his own great, brown hands, that lay on the edge of the table.

"Signed confession," repeated Speedy.

"I'll see you dead first," exploded Simmons.

"I told you that you'd never get it out of him, Speedy," said Al Dupray, shaking his weary head.

"Then we'll hang him in his own house," said Speedy. "We'll hang him up to his own ceiling. And we'll do it now."

"You won't. That's not your line, Speedy," said Simmons. "I know you too well for that. You can't bluff me, boys! You wouldn't do a murder that would outlaw the lot of you!"

"Murder?" said Speedy. "It will pass as a suicide. When they find you, they'll find your hands free, and your signed confession lying on the table."

"My signed confession? And how might you be getting that out of me?" asked Simmons, squinting his eyes. "Besides, I never done the job."

"Don't be a fool, Simmons," said Speedy, as calmly as ever. "The fact is that you killed Tom Older, and now conscience has got hold of you, and you'll hang yourself, you poor devil, and leave your signed confession lying here on the table!"

'You're gonna drive me crazy, are you? Think I'm fool enough to write out a confession?" asked Simmons.

Speedy smiled.

"I'll write it for you, brother," he said. "I'm a penman, Simmons. You seem to have heard so much about me, that perhaps you've heard that, too."

Simmons stared long and earnestly. Conviction was dawning slowly in his eyes, and now his mouth dropped open, yet it was a moment before he could speak.

"What would you write down in that there confession?" he asked. "Why, nobody would believe it. Everybody knows that I was a good friend of Tom Older."

"That's the point of it," said Speedy. "When you dropped in on Tom at his camp, he was so sure that you were his friend, that he even showed you the sample and the place he chipped it. Then he sat down beside the fire and talked, warmed his hands at it, while you picked up the ax to get more wood and, while you stood there behind him, it came into your mind that it would be an easy thing to put him out of the way. You remembered how he'd told you of Dupray's discontent. Other people knew that young Al was dissatisfied, also. Therefore, the impulse came over you in a twinkling.

You're not a young man. Before long, you'd have begun to get old and stiff. So you lifted the ax and—"

"Stop!" gasped Simmons. "Where were you hiding, Speedy, that you seen it?"

He collected himself, instantly.

"I mean," he said. "I mean to say that there ain't a word of truth in that lingo!"

"You can write out the confession and go to jail," said Speedy, still very calm and steady, "and there you can take your chances with the law, or else we'll hang you up here, man, and leave every sign to make the world sure that you committed suicide out of a guilty conscience."

He nodded to Slim Malone.

"You have the rope, Slim, I think," said he.

"It's here," said Malone.

He looked up toward the ceiling, at the big iron hook projecting downward, from which a lamp had probably once been suspended.

"It's all right," said Speedy. "We won't have to use it, or will we, Simmons?"

The gentleness of his voice caused a shudder of horror to sweep through the big body of Simmons.

Suddenly he said: "I'll write it! It was the damned ax! If only I hadn't laid my hands on it!"

"You'd better be drifting, Slim," said Speedy, after a time, while the pen was still scratching.

Slim Malone took off his hat and smoothed his rust-colored hair.

Then he grinned. "I suppose they want me more'n ever," he suggested. "More for the jailbreak, now, than for what I did before, eh?"

"I suppose so," said Speedy. "That was a good turn you did me in the jail, Slim. I'll remember it."

Slim Malone drew up his slender, athletic body to its full height.

"Why, Speedy, it was worth it," he said, "just for the pleasure of seein' how you handled that job there in the jail. I call it pretty slick. So long, old man."

"So long," said Speedy. "Remember me, partner. You and I could ride some trail together, one of these days."

"Just say my name out loud whenever you want me," answered Malone, "and I'll manage to hear it and come on the dead run. So long again. Good-by, Dupray. I'm glad you're out of this here mess."

But Dupray was asleep in his chair!

Malone did not waken him. He simply stepped through the door and sped down the steps. A moment later, they heard the snort of his horse, and the thumping of hoofs as it galloped away through the night.

Still the pen of Simmons scratched on and on. He sweated, not with agony at the words which he was forced to write, but with the labor of committing them to the paper. He bit his lip and grunted, strained and finally looked up with a sigh of relief.

"That's about all, I guess," said he, and added: "Wanta read it over?"

"I've read it already," said Speedy, picking it up. "It will do well enough. I read upside down, as you scrawled it."

"You're full of tricks," muttered Simmons. "You'll trick yourself into the hottest part of hell, one of these days!"

He lifted his head again. Horses had swept up the road and now they stopped in front of the house.

"That's probably the deputy sheriff," said Speedy, "come to catch Dupray and me, but he'll be glad to have you instead!"

# 42

Now, for a moment, silence came over that room. Al Dupray was still sunk in sleep. The hand of Simmons went up to his throat, and his eyes gradually closed as he spoke, breaking the silence:

"It's kind of a funny thing; the way I've come into this. I mean, it was the ax, the feel of it in my hand. It was like the ax did the trick, and not my hand that had hold of it. It's kind of funny."

There was a light, crackling sound, outside the house.

"They're on the veranda, now, and they're going to rush in and surprise us, pretty soon," said Speedy.

He smiled at that, the smile twisting all to one side on account of the pull of the imitation scar that was on his face.

Only a moment more, then through the window, came the voice of the young deputy sheriff, Stewart Osgood, saying: "Up with your hands, Speedy. We got you covered from this here window, and from the door of the hall. We got Dupray, too. Up with your hands, or I'll let you have it!"

Speedy did not raise his hands. He did not turn his head, even, but said: "That's all right, Osgood. You're going to get enough out of this to make you a full sheriff at the next election, but don't think that you're going to get it out of me. Keep me covered, and send your men in."

There is incalculable force in the power of quiet calm and self-control. Deputy Sheriff Osgood muttered a few orders, and his men stalked into the room, their guns ready.

They covered Speedy and Dupray; but Simmons made no move to break away, for he saw that Speedy's eyes were upon him, something as the eyes of a hunting cat might be upon its prey, conveniently near.

Al Dupray was unaware of the intrusion. He simply slumped forward in his chair and, burying his face in his arms on the top of the table, he continued to sleep the sleep of utter exhaustion.

"Pick up that paper," said Speedy, to the first man who had entered, and that was none other than his friend the guard of the jail.

The man obeyed. His voice went slowly over the words of the confession; before it ended, Stewart Osgood was standing in the room, listening with a frown of wonder.

At the end, not one of them was heeding Speedy or Al Dupray, after whom they had ridden so hard and so successfully that night. Their guns were pointing toward Pete Simmons, instead.

He jumped out of his chair at last, and cried out: "It's all a lie!"

"It's wrote in your own hand," said Osgood, sternly.

"I had to write it. These two devils made me at the point of a gun," said Simmons. "Speedy, he swore that otherwise they'd hang me, and he'd forge my confession, and go and leave it here, like I was a suicide.''

His voice trailed away and stopped. For his own guilt closed over his throat. He could not help feeling that the confession was not more visible in his written words than in his face at that moment.

"Well," said Osgood. "I guess that's about all you wanta say now, Simmons."

"D'you mean that you'll take this serious?" demanded Simmons. "D'you mean that a thug like Speedy, and a killer like Dupray, out of murderous blood—"

Al Dupray stirred and groaned in his sleep. That sound stopped the voice of Simmons in the midst of his protest and, looking about him, he saw contempt, disgust, horror, in every face among the posse.

"What I'm thinking of," said Osgood, "is that poor Tom Older was a friend of yours. He was an old bunkie. And yet you'd murder him with an ax! It makes me sick. You're under arrest, Simmons. Anything more that you say may be used agin' you in the law courts."

He stepped to Simmons, and clamped the handcuffs over his big brown wrists. The man sank back in his chair, with a gasping groan.

Even this did not awaken Dupray.

"You and Dupray, Speedy," said Osgood, "will have to come back to the town till I get a court order that frees you. There's gonna be some kind of a charge agin' you, for breaking jail—well, and turning Slim Malone loose. I reckon that there won't be any charge, though, for makin' a fool of me. That's throwed in free and extra, I guess!"

"What else could I do, Osgood, but work on you?" said Speedy. "I had to get into the jail, and how else could I do it?"

"I dunno," said Osgood. "And I ain't so sad about it, neither. I ain't the first ordinary gent that's been buffaloed by you, and I reckon that I won't be the last, neither. I'd take more than that to keep from hanging the wrong man, even if he is a Dupray."

He looked down at the sleeping form of the young man and added, with a sudden compassion: "Doggone me, but we used him rough. It's the last time that the third degree is ever used in Clausen, and you can believe that, if you want to!''

"I believe it," said Speedy.

"Wake him up," ordered the deputy sheriff. "Let him come along with us, Speedy. You've gotta go back."

"Let him stay out on parole with me, till tomorow," answered Speedy. "I'll promise to bring him back when he's had his sleep."

The sheriff hesitated. Then, nodding, he observed: "They say that your word is enough for any man in your part of the country, and I guess that your part of the country is as good as mine. I'll trust you to show up with him tomorrow by noon, say?"

"Right," answered Speedy.

So it was that Al Dupray slept all through that scene which removed Pete Simmons from the house and started that unhappy man back toward the town of Clausen and a life sentence!

Speedy, when he heard the hoofbeats depart, roused Dupray, and got him staggering, like a child, to the bed; saw him topple over, straightened out his legs, pulled off his coat and boots without completely waking him, and then pulled a pair of blankets over him.

After that, he went to the top of the hill behind the house, brought the pair of horses down to the shed and fed them.

For his own part, he was not sleepy. There was in him an ability to store up energy and sleep in quiet times that served him well in days of need, when his reserve strength had to be drawn upon over a considerable period. It served him now and, coming back to the shack of Simmons, he kindled a fire in the stove, boiled some coffee, fried some bacon, and sat down with this and a cold pone to an appetizing, if small meal.

Later, still, he washed and scrubbed from his face, hands and body the dark stain which had covered it, using laundry soap, hot water in a galvanized iron laundry tub, and a certain chemical which he took out of a small vial in his pocket.

The dawn came before he had finished all of this work, and he went back to look at Dupray, who was still sleeping soundly.

There was no other bed in the place. Speedy, therefore, went to the table at which Simmons had sat to write his confession, kicked off his boots and, stretching himself on the table, without so much as a blanket under him for cushion or over him for warmth, he closed his eyes and was instantly asleep.

He slept till well on in the morning, and then awoke automatically, as though an alarm had rung in his ears.

Walking back to the other room, he found that Dupray was just waking up, yawning prodigiously as he sat up on the side of his bunk.

He leaped to his feet at the sight of Speedy.

"You, Speedy!" he began.

"It's all right. Take it easy," said Speedy.

"Where are we, I mean?" he said confusedly.

"We're in Simmons's house. You remember back a ways. He wrote out his confession, signed it, and Osgood and a posse came here for us, and went away with Simmons, instead."

"Great Scott!" exclaimed Dupray. "How did I manage to sleep through all of that?"

"An easy conscience, perhaps," suggested Speedy, rather dryly.

Dupray glanced sharply aside at him but, making no answer, he sat down again to pull on his boots.

Speedy worked up a new fire and cooked a second breakfast. In silence he cooked and in silence they ate, for a great cloud seemed to have enveloped the mind of young Dupray.

Finally, over his second cup of coffee, he said: "Look here, Speedy, what's on your mind? You're keeping something back!"

"Only that you're going back to Clausen with me today," said Speedy.

"Going back?" exclaimed young Dupray. "Why should I go back? I'm free, now, if they've got Simmons for that job."

"I promised the sheriff that I'd bring you in," said Speedy.

The sight of his calm face suddenly seemed to madden Al Dupray. He grew ugly; for an instant he looked not like the nephew but the very son of that Charley Dupray who was Speedy's greatest enemy.

"The hell you did," Al Dupray shouted out. "And who are you to promise the sheriff anything from me? I'll handle myself, thanks!"

Speedy rose from the table and went to the window, through which he stared out over the valley, glistening under the morning sun. There he waited, until presently the voice of the young man said, just at his shoulder: "I'm sorry. I was a fool. I clean forgot."

"Don't be apologizing," said Speedy. "If you're ready to go, we'll start now."

"Only," said Dupray, "I dunno about going back to Clausen. I ain't liked there. I dunno that I'm liked anywhere, but particular in Clausen, they always hated me!"

"Why should they?" asked Speedy.

"My name's Dupray. That's enough," said Al, his face wrinkling at the disagreeable thought.

"You've got a new position, now," said Speedy. "They called you a murderer. Now, instead of that, they find out that you're an honest man, with something that means more than honesty."

"What's that?" asked Dupray, humbly.

"Money," said Speedy. "You have the mine, now. Your claim to it is as clean as a whistle."

"By thunder," said Dupray, "I'd clean forgot about that. But now that I'm gonna be cleared, why, of course, it's mine."

He lifted his head with a jerk and laughed. Then he snapped his fingers.

"Some of 'em can look up to me now!" he said. "I'll snap my whip, and they can jump!"

He snapped his fingers, in token of the good time to come.

Then, changing his mind quickly, he said: "Look here, Speedy."

"All right," said Speedy. "Look at what?"

"Except for you, I'd be closer to hanging by the length of one night, instead of farther away from it. I owe it to you."

"You owe it to your uncle," said Speedy. "You don't owe anything to me."

The young man laughed. "You wanta put it that way," said he, "but the fact is, Speedy, that you saved me. Well, I was partners with poor Tom Older; though it's true that I wrangled a good bit with him, I was fond of him. He was a salty old bird, I can tell you, and honest, too. He was willing to trust a Dupray, for one thing.''

His face darkened, as he said this, and then he continued slowly: "But with Older out of the picture, there's something remaining, Speedy. Half of that mine belongs to me, but I want the other half to belong to you.''

Speedy shook his head.

"I can't take it,'' said he.

"Because you can't take anything from a Dupray, eh?'' demanded the youth.

"I didn't say that.''

"You meant it, though.''

"Al,'' said Speedy, "it's not because you're a Dupray, but because of two things. The first is, there's blood on it, Older's blood. It's a queer freak with me, but I hate blood money. The second thing is, you don't owe any gratitude to me. You owe it to your uncle.''

Al Dupray blinked, and waited for the explanation. And Speedy went on, slowly and solemnly: "If I'd heard of you being in prison, before, I would have been glad of it. I would have been glad to know that another Dupray was to die. You see? But your uncle came and caught me off base. Away off base and up in the air. I was in his hand, and three other friends of mine were in his hand, too. He only had to scratch a match in a grain field. And you know that he hates me, Al.''

Dupray nodded. His eyes, animal bright and quick, kept playing over the face of Speedy, as though trying to find a hidden solution behind his words and expression.

Then he said: "Doggone me, Speedy, I can't imagine why he didn't scratch the match, then. I know that he's hated you, all right! What would keep him from bumping you off? What's the answer?''

He waited eagerly, hanging upon the answer.

And Speedy said: "Because he loves you, Al, and thought I might be able to help you.''

Al Dupray blinked and winced.

Still his eyes roved, as though the answer were not entire

and satisfying. At last Speedy said: "About the mine, if you think that anything should be given away, remember Tom Older, your grubstake partner. Even that hound, Simmons, was going to give some money in the name of Older. Why don't you give fifty cents out of every dollar the mine makes for you and invest it in some charity, in Tom Older's name?"

Dupray caught in his breath. Then he gasped: "Jiminy, Speedy, everybody would think I'd gone crazy, wouldn't they? But why not? Just to give 'em a slam in the eye!"

# 43

They rode into the town of Clausen, shoulder to shoulder, and just before noon they entered the long, winding, main street of the town.

A whisper and a rumor ran before them. People hurried to windows and doors. Little children appeared by magic and trooped about.

"Look around," said Speedy, to his companion. "If those people seemed to hate you before, don't they seem to be changing their minds, just now?"

Al Dupray lifted his head, and breathed more deeply once more.

"It looks kind of like a new world, that I never seen before, Speedy," he declared. "You sort of opened the door of it to me!"

"Your uncle did," insisted Speedy. "He gave me up. And he'd rather have had the best blood out of my heart than anything in the world. You're the only thing that makes a bigger difference to him!"

"Yeah?" murmured the boy, bewildered. "And that's a funny thing, too." He added: "You know how it is, I never heard from Uncle Charley much, except somebody appears in the middle of the night and drops a letter into my hand, then slides off. In the letter there's just a few words that say: 'Here's some of the velvet, so you can spend it fast! Good luck.' That's the way that one of his letters would go. I never seen his face, myself, more'n half a dozen times, and he was never very doggone kind, at that. Look a-here, Speedy, d'you think that I look like him?''

There was a world of anxiety in him. And Speedy answered, briefly: ''You do.''

''Do I?'' groaned the young man.

''You look like the best part of him,'' said Speedy.

''Whacha mean by that?'' said Al Dupray.

''The Duprays are an old family, and they used to be a good one,'' said Speedy. ''And they ought to be a good one again. They've gone wild, and that's all.''

Dupray stared before him with a wretched face.

''Bad blood!'' he muttered.

Or, at least, that was what the words seemed to be, to the acute ear of Speedy, who answered: ''What d'you mean by bad blood?''

''Like back there in Simmons's shack—after all that you'd done for me,'' said Dupray, gloomily, ''but this morning when I thought that you were sort of ordering me around, why, in another minute I could've killed you!''

''Take hold of this idea, partner,'' said Speedy.

''Yes?'' said Al, eagerly.

''Listen to me, now. When you see a colt in the corral that drives the rest of the horses around, you may say to yourself that it's not the handsomest of the lot, and it's not the biggest. But you've an idea, as a rule, that that horse has bottom to it. Am I wrong?''

''No, you're dead right,'' muttered Al.

''Well, when that colt grows up, it's likely to need some handling,'' said Speedy, ''or else it will begin to go wrong, and it'll go wrong as soon as the people that handle it think it's wrong. Because your horse is going to be as bad, or twice as bad, as you let yourself think it is.''

''Yes, that's true, and I sort of see what you mean,'' said Dupray. ''I see right through the deal. Oh, Speedy, you've got a brain in your head.''

His enthusiasm was growing.

''You've grown up thinking that there was bad blood in you,'' said Speedy. ''What does that bad blood amount to?''

''Murder!'' broke out Al Dupray, in a low, choking voice.

"Damnable, black murder, and lots of it. That's what's been in my blood, and my father's blood before me, and his father before him."

In the exquisite perfection of his pain, he grinned, as though squinting at the sun.

"Murder, you say? There's something else, though," said Speedy.

"What else?" groaned Al Dupray. "There's murder, Speedy, and there's been murder in me. There was murder in me this very morning, and for the only man in the world, about, that's ever tried to do a kind thing for me."

"Besides murder," said Speedy, "there's strength and courage. You, Al, you never cried 'enough' in your life, not even when a bigger boy was thumping you!"

"How did you know that?" asked Al, suddenly wide of eye.

"I know it because I know that you're a Dupray," said Speedy.

"Do you?" gasped Al.

"Yes. And besides, I know that you never will say 'enough.' No Dupray ever surrenders. Why, an army of a thousand Duprays would conquer the whole world, if they'd fight shoulder to shoulder."

"A thousand Duprays?" repeated the young man. "That'd be an ugly mess, all right."

He laughed a little, with excitement in his eyes.

"Then," said Speedy, "every Dupray has endurance. He can handle his body as though it were iron. A Dupray will ride or walk farther, climb higher, stand more heat or cold, fight harder, starve longer, and never say die. The fellow who has the luck to be born a Dupray is born a thoroughbred. Between him and other people, there's the difference that there is between a Kentucky thoroughbred and a plow horse."

"Would you say that?" said Al.

"I would say it, and I am saying it. I'd bet on a Dupray any day."

"You'd bet on a Dupray," said the boy, slowly, "to break the law, and to die before he'd let himself be put in prison for it. That's how you'd bet on a Dupray."

"It's true. The whole lot of the Duprays have been too hot

under the collar all the time,'' said Speedy. ''That's what they've been. But you, Al, have had a chance to cool off. You'll find that you've a better temper than the rest. You're the sort of diamond that can cut diamond. Use yourself right. Respect yourself as much as I respect you, and you'll surely rule the roost.''

Al Dupray said nothing, but his eyes were blazing, and there was on his face such a smile as no man had seen there before.

Suddenly Speedy said: ''Who was your mother, Al?''

''Mother? What's she got to do with it?'' asked Al Dupray, suddenly angry.

''She's your mother,'' said Speedy. ''That's what she has to do with you. Was a wrong thing ever whispered about her?''

''No!'' said Al Dupray, with vehemence. ''Whacha mean?''

''Then remember that your blood is half hers, and no man ever dared to so much as whisper a wrong thing about your mother! Here's the jail, Al. We turn in here and pay a call, I think. We may even have lunch in a cell, for all I know. I hope they have a good cook.''

Al Dupray was suddenly laughing, as he swung down from his horse and went up toward the jail, arm in arm with his companion.

Stewart Osgood met them at the door of the jail and brought them straight to his office.

''I've got the judge here,'' he was saying. ''I dunno how far I can go, but the judge, he knows. I was watchin' the sun, and kind of wondering if you'd be in, right on time, Speedy, and the kid along with you.''

He heaved a sigh, as though a great weight had just been removed from his mind. Then, leading the way, he opened the door and admitted them to his office, where the gray-headed judge was sitting, a stern, quiet man, with a face that had braved many troubles.

''Here they are,'' said the deputy sheriff. ''I don't want to have you waste much of your time. I know that you're a busy man, Judge Welch; but I'm only wondering, after all, if it was a jailbreak. It's true that we were holdin' Al Dupray on a wrong charge, but a jailbreak's a jailbreak. Then, they let out

Malone. We weren't holding Malone for nothing much, but he was turned loose.''

"The law can go hang," said the Honorable John J. Welch. "I could have told you last night that you'd be a fool to arrest either of 'em. But I wanted to see Speedy, face to face, and here he is—here he is.''

He nodded to Al Dupray. Speedy he gripped by the hand, and deliberately turned him toward the window light, as a father might turn the face of his son.

Holding the hand of the younger man still, he said: "It was a good thing and a great thing and a brave thing, Speedy— since you won't tell us your true name. No other man in the world, I think, could have done it. I'm glad to have seen your face. I've a boy at home, Speedy, that may grow up to look like you; but if he grows up to be like you in more than looks, may Fate help him as much as I'll admire him!''

## 44

Arriving at the house of John Wilson, William Cort flung himself from his horse without tethering it. He paused only long enough to throw the reins, then he ran in through the kitchen door. There he found, not Jessica Wilson, but the amazed cook and, stamping into the front of the house, came at length upon the two Wilsons. They rose up with frightened faces before him.

"He's done it," gasped William Cort, falling exhausted into a chair. "He's freed Al Dupray from the jail. I sent the telegram we agreed on, you know. We thought that it would be a way of heading Speedy off from terrible trouble, but he was already inside the jail. I don't know just how he wangled it, but he did the job, and he's managed to get Al Dupray loose. Not only that, but it turns out that young Al was wrongly accused, and it was proved by Speedy. He found the real killer and made him confess.

"The town of Clausen is burning up with excitement. Young Al Dupray has made a talk to the best men of the town and told 'em that he's giving half the profits of his mine, and it's a rich one, too, to any charity in the place. And why d'you think he's doing it? Because, he says, Speedy has taken a rope from around his neck, but chiefly out of regard for the 'love and kindness'—yes, sir, those are the words!—the love and kindness of his uncle, Charley Dupray, who got Speedy interested in the business. It's the darnedest thing that I've ever seen in a newspaper.

"I rode my horse almost into the ground to get out here to you and tell you about it. Besides, I want to be here when we explain to Speedy why we sent a telegram that might have got him into such hot water, instead of saving him from burning his fingers, as we figured it! He ought to be here almost any time, if he rides back this way, and this is the way he's pretty sure to ride."

Not three miles away, in a narrow glen coming out of the hills, Speedy at that moment was jogging his mustang, sleepily, horse and rider hanging their heads a little, with the heat of the sun pouring down steadily upon them.

But for all the somnolence of his mood, the warmth and sleep that were soaking through his body and his spirit, he was instantly aware of the shadow that moved behind one of the trees.

He checked the mustang instantly and was off its back in a flash, its body between him and possible danger.

Then said the harsh, ringing voice of Charley Dupray: "It's all right, Speedy!"

Then, the great Dupray in person appeared from among the trees, leading after him a lofty thoroughbred with wide, shining forehead, starred with white, and the eye of a deer, ready for flight.

The beauty of the animal and the ugliness of the white, frog-face of the man worked strangely in the mind of Speedy. He stepped out in front of his mustang.

"Hello, Dupray," said he.

Dupray waved a hand.

"Speedy," he said, "we've burned up ten of the thirty-day truce. I'm thinking that I'd like to make it longer."

Speedy shrugged his shoulders.

"You think so now," he suggested. "But you'll change

your mind, later on. You'll remember a few of the other old days, and they'll burn you up."

"Would you trust me, Speedy, if I gave you my word?" asked Dupray, curiously.

"No," said Speedy, "if you swore on all the Bibles in the world."

"You wouldn't trust me, eh?"

"No," said Speedy.

The other nodded and seemed to take no offense.

"Maybe you're right," said he. "I don't know. Just now I think that maybe I could go straight, as far as you're concerned. You've done a pretty big job for me, Speedy."

The latter waved his hand in turn to banish the suggestion of kindness.

"All in the day's work," he said.

"There's something else, though, that's not in the day's work," said Charley Dupray.

"What's that?"

"This," said Dupray. "And if you're not behind the writing of the best thing that ever came to me, more than gold or diamonds, I'll eat my own heart out with my own teeth. Look at this!"

He held out a square of paper and Speedy, unfolding it, read:

DEAR UNCLE CHARLEY: By this time you know that Speedy has got me freed and put me right before the world, so right that people here in Clausen seem to think that my name may not be Dupray after all. But I'm going to teach them that it is Dupray—only, the sort of a Dupray that they don't expect, the sort of a Dupray that you could be, if you hadn't chosen the other way of living. But, whatever I am, I'll owe it to you, and never forget you while there's blood in me.

Your affectionate nephew,                                    Al